GRAVE MISTAKE

KATE ALLENTON

Dedicated to Hollie Mae
You are a true blessing and welcome new addition to the
family. May you always follow your dreams and your
heart.

And

Dedicated in Loving memory of Ed Warnick
A loving husband, father, father-in-law, grandfather, and
friend. Your presence will be truly missed.
1947 – 2021

A funeral was a time to say goodbye.

Ryley's attendance wasn't so cut and dried.

Love and light were good and all that, but so were peace and sleep. And Ryley's well-being wasn't a toy to be played with. Any lingering souls sticking around had the potential to hold Ryley's sleep hostage. And that was not good for anyone.

From the relative safety of her car, Ryley stared across the funeral parking lot to the chapel, where mourners were already starting to congregate.

Colors on the stained-glass windows shimmered in red, blue, and green hues in the morning sun. The colors were a direct contrast to the large white concrete building. The place looked peaceful to the untrained eye.

Looks could be deceiving. She'd learned that the hard way.

The Creepy Crawlies slithered like spiders over tombstones in the distance. They were a mix between shadow people and animals being lured by the smell of death the way a dog might when it smelled a grilling steak. They were bad news for the dead, sniffing out lingering souls and attacking like a starved man in front of a mouthwatering steak. Luckily, they were still far enough away they couldn't smell the newly departed teen.

There was still time to save her soul.

Ryley's car idled as she ran through her mental list.

"Strays are not my friend. Avoid eye contact."

That was a hard and fast rule she couldn't break. An occupational hazard that was sometimes hard to avoid when the dead appeared more alive than the living.

"I can't save everyone," she reaffirmed with a stubborn shake of her head.

She rubbed her hands together, psyching herself up for this personal mission.

Ryley's pep talks were becoming more frequent now that her secret hobby of funeral crashing had been outed by the media. Her previous welcome at funerals was now tainted with unease and gossip.

"Get in, if the teen's spirit is still lingering, then touch her arm to send her into the light."

Ryley was a bully in the spirit world. One touch of a dead body whose spirit lingered nearby and it was bon voyage, baby. Don't let the pearly gates hit you in the ass on your way into heaven.

She didn't care if the newly departed would rather stay and haunt the living; she wouldn't let them. There was no room for banter. Not even for the old-timers who promised words of wisdom and life lessons.

They all had to go. Ryley didn't play favorites, although she'd never turn down a bribe that included the location of hidden money or jewels.

The scent of floral perfume tickled Ryley's nose as a chill swept over her body. It was always the first sign that she was no longer alone.

"Quit being a wuss and go take care of business," Stretch's ghostly apparition said, appearing in the backseat.

Catherine Floyd, or Stretch, as the ghostly woman liked to be called, had been a stripper in life and also the mother of Eli Floyd, the criminal that

Ryley, at the tender of age five, helped to put behind bars. Stretch had been following Ryley around ever since, offering a free education into everything undead while making Ryley her new best friend.

She was a bad influence, and Ryley loved her for it. Most times. It's not like she could send her into the great beyond. Not without access to touch Stretch's bones. Even if she could, she wasn't sure she would send the woman away.

"That teen looks like she's going to be a ton of trouble if I can't get her into the light." Ryley sighed. Her bravado slowly dissipated like air from a leaky tire. Her stomach tightened in unease.

Stretch appeared in the front seat. *"You can handle her. I have faith."*

Faith wasn't a luxury Ryley could afford. She'd once had faith in a system that could hide her and keep her safe. She'd had faith in medical professionals that could save her mother's life. Both had failed miserably.

"Why don't you go do some recon and tell me if it's an open casket?" Ryley nodded toward the chapel.

"I thought you'd never ask." Stretch grinned as she disappeared.

At five, Ryley had witnessed a murder and then tried to kill her dad.

At six, she'd testified and sent a man to prison, got a new identity, and picked up the ghostly stripper as a best friend.

Her therapist said those were her formative years, before she'd really had a choice. Once she reached the age to know better, she simply didn't care and picked which vices would keep her alive.

So, this wasn't all her fault. Not really.

Having a best friend like Stretch had its perks. Spying was only one of them.

Forming goosebumps announced Stretch's return to the car. *"This one should be a piece of cake."*

Ryley had made the mistake of believing that before.

"There's an open casket. Even if you have to tackle everyone in your way to get to the body, you should be able to move this girl into the light."

"Good to know." The tension in Ryley's shoulders started to give way.

"And be quick about it. I know when you leave here that you plan to go see your hot brother before he goes to court, and I'm in dire need of some eye candy."

"You sure you don't want to hitch a ride with the teen? I'm sure they'll let you reincarnate."

"Hah." The sharp laugh was followed with a deadpanned look. "Could you imagine what they'd send me back as? I'd probably be a rat, or worse."

A slow smile split Ryley's lips as she picked up the white rose from the center console.

"But what if it was something much better?" Ryley asked.

"It sounds like you're trying to get rid of me." Stretch balked.

Maybe. "Now, why would I do that?"

"You'd miss me," Stretch said matter-of-factly.

"If you say so." Ryley tried to hide the humor in her eyes.

"Go take care of business so we can get a move on," Stretch said with a roll of her eyes before she vanished again.

Ryley sighed and glanced once more at the name in the newspaper for the funeral she was attending. Tessa Murphy, nineteen years old.

Ryley stepped out of the car and smoothed the wrinkles out of her black skirt. Taking a deep breath, she turned her gaze to the funeral home door and kept it locked on the target, refusing to make eye contact with the newly departed young girl.

She could do this. She didn't have a choice.

Stretch had better not be lying.

No, she wouldn't have lied. Would she?

She totally would, just to watch Ryley squirm.

The momentary hesitation stirred the butterflies in her stomach back to life.

2

Cigarette smoke lingered in the air as a couple of men in the distance talked on the sidewalk. Hushed whispers started as she passed another group of adults. Their disapproving look told her at least one person in this group had read the newspaper and knew Ryley didn't belong.

Her welcome was waning. She was sure of that.

In the lobby, a table sat just outside the chapel door, holding the registry and copies of the program. She grabbed a program to add to her collection of souvenirs but bypassed the registry. She never left proof of her attendance.

Soft music was playing as she stepped into the chapel. A couple of seated people were dabbing at their teary eyes. Others were in murmured conversation. Pews creaked as people claimed their spots. The floral scent from an array of fresh flower arrangements filled the room.

The family stood near the end of the casket, speaking with a pastor. The man of God had his hand on the father's arm, offering support. The mother had her arm wrapped around another young adult woman cuddling a baby in her arms. Both women comforting each other looked numb.

Ryley would be, too, if she didn't have this gift. Death wasn't the end; it was a transition.

The casket lay open, offering a glimpse of the college-aged girl inside. A simple, quick touch was all Ryley would need to see how Tessa had died, to move her along. No fuss.

One quick second was all she'd need.

Tessa appeared in the corner, watching everyone as if still in a state of shock and debating what to do about her predicament. Her brown shoulder-length hair lay in tangles on her head, in need of a brush. The torn shirt showed signs of dried blood. Dirt covered her pale face, and gashes in her arms and neck showed where she'd been bleeding.

She hadn't died a peaceful death.

Tessa momentarily met Ryley's gaze.

Ryley dropped her gaze to the rose in her hand and sniffed, averting the potential mishap.

Stay on target. No getting derailed. We aren't taking another stray home.

Whispers filtered up the aisle. A line was forming to say their goodbyes at the casket. Ryley waited patiently behind a group of teens.

"I heard she was using drugs."

"I heard she dropped out of college because she was failing."

"Probably because of the drugs," another girl added.

Some friends these people were, that were already starting rumors without knowing the truth.

"I don't know, but I passed her that morning, and she looked tired. Maybe she just fell asleep at the wheel."

Finally, a rational explanation. Maybe that girl really was Tessa's friend, unlike the others in attendance.

"Because of the drugs," the other person added.

They all nodded in unison.

Ryley held in her irritated sigh. She'd know one way or another as soon as she touched Tessa. Maybe Ryley would stop to tell these girls the truth.

Maybe not.

"You know, I heard she's been sneaking around."

"Well, I know firsthand she's been hanging out with the wrong crowd. I've seen her coming out of Deadheads, and you know the scum that hangs out in that bar."

Ryley frowned, hearing the reference to Deadheads. The negative energy of the people in that place seeped out in waves.

Tessa's spirit moved closer to her family. They were still conversing with the pastor. She was adamantly trying to get their attention by getting in the middle of the group and putting her face close to the others, yelling at them all.

The distraught family didn't have a clue that their dead daughter lingered nearby.

A slideshow on the screen showed happier times in Tessa's life. A life that had been cut way too short.

"Funeral crashing again, I see." Henry's whispered voice startled her.

Henry was new to town and working as an assistant to Father James, whose eulogies Ryley enjoyed best. She'd met him a couple months back. Too bad Father Henry wasn't the one presiding over this one. It would have made things easier. He understood Ryley's quirks, unlike the Catholic Pastor standing at the front of the room.

"Have you reverted to stalking me?" Ryley teased.

Henry's cheeks tinted. "Are you coming or going?"

"Both," Ryley said with a strained smile. "Just here to pay my respects, and then I'm leaving. Can't stay for the eulogy."

"I see. I guess in the world of funeral crashing, that's considered doing a drive-by," he said, gesturing toward the front of the room.

"Isn't it illegal or something for you to be attending the funeral of another clergyman? I thought you religious guys of different denominations didn't play well together in the sandbox."

Henry chuckled. "I'm a lawbreaker."

"I kind of doubt that." Ryley grinned.

"I'm off the clock. This one's personal. I'm friends with the family, so I'm here to show them my respect too. Come on; we can say a quick prayer together."

"You sure you want to be seen with me? I'll ruin your reputation so badly that even the good Lord won't be able to repair it. You'll have to wear a red robe to services instead of white," Ryley said, glancing around the pews to the people already staring in her direction and whispering. "Looks like it's already starting."

The gossip had started two funerals ago when

13

Ryley made the news when she'd inherited Old Man Wilson's fortune without even knowing the guy, all because she'd been the only one to attend his funeral.

"Who's to say they aren't staring at me?" Henry teased. "You know I am single and new in town."

She grinned. Henry was wrong, of course, but she could pretend and be delusional just as easily as he could, if not better.

Glendale Pike wasn't a metropolis, but it was a big enough city to get lost in and was still growing every day. The shopping and pristine lakes brought fishers and tourist in from miles away. Henry was just one of the latest transplants.

He was a good-looking guy. Strong and tall. He exuded an unusual calmness. Maybe he might be interested in providing her with some personal Zen? She wouldn't be opposed to leaving money on the bedside table every time she visited.

She met Tessa's gaze again.

Stay on target. Her debauchery would have to wait, or just maybe she could give these people something else to talk about. Something to forget the real reason she'd attended.

"Let me know when you want to give them

something really juicy to talk about." Ryley ran her fingers suggestively up Henry's chest, batting her eyes with an evil grin.

He rested his hand over hers, stopping the action. "This might not be an appropriate time."

"Life is short, Henry. You've got to have fun while you can." She chuckled as the line moved. The group of gossipers started moving ahead in twos, taking their time.

"I bet you tease all the boys," Henry whispered.

"Only the ones deemed off-limits." She shrugged.

If her statement bothered Henry, he didn't let on. His straightlaced expression didn't give away his reaction.

"Relax, I'm teasing." Sort of. She chuckled. She'd have to learn to master her own reactions.

It was almost her turn.

The parents and the pastor were deep in conversation as the mother dabbed her eyes.

Ryley made it to the very first pew. The casket and Tessa's body were within reach and so close that Ryley could almost feel the victory.

As the last girls in the gossip group approached, the pastor frowned and stepped away from the family, blocking Ryley's path. "You don't belong here. I know who you are. I read about you in the paper, and you most certainly don't know this family."

Ryley swallowed hard. "I just came to pay my respects. I don't want any trouble."

3

"Marvin, do you know this girl?" the pastor asked Tessa's father.

Ryley didn't have time for this.

She slowly lowered the rose in her hand before she hit the pastor with it and made a break for the casket. No matter how necessary the move, it most certainly would leave a bad mark on her ethereal record.

"No, Pastor Peterson. She wasn't a friend of Tessa's."

"I think you need to leave, young lady. You're intruding on an emotional moment for these people," Pastor Peterson said, gesturing in a circle for her to turn around and go back up the aisle.

"I just wanted to leave a parting rose and show my respects like everyone else."

"You aren't welcome here." He narrowed his eyes at Ryley before turning his disapproving look toward Henry as if Henry had a hand in Ryley's actions.

"All of God's children are capable of grieving." Henry tried to de-escalate the situation.

"Yeah, well, if the papers are to be believed, Tessa's spirit will do better without this woman's respect. Please leave," Pastor Peterson said with a stiff jab in the air toward the door.

Tessa's spirit moved closer, and she frowned as she looked at the pastor and then Ryley.

Unavoidable contact was made.

Son of a mother, freakin', frackin'... Ryley narrowed her eyes at Pastor Peterson. She could have moved Tessa on had he not stepped in her way. "Judging people isn't very saintly of you, now is it, Pastor Peterson?"

Henry's hand landed on Ryley's arm as if he knew she was about to make a scene. One that would get out of hand really quick. "Ryley, how about you give me the rose. I'll leave it for you and say a prayer for both of us."

The last thing she wanted to do was concede to

this man and lose her chance of moving Tessa along. Didn't he realize she was just trying to help save a soul?

They practically had the same job.

"Just this once." Henry tried to soothe.

Ryley pursed her lips together, biting back her argument. She slapped the rose into Henry's hand. Meeting the mother's gaze, she reined in her anger, maintaining her inner calm. "I am sorry for your loss."

A smile slipped onto the pastor's face.

"Asshat," Ryley grumbled beneath her breath and spun on her heels. The heaviness of watchful eyes followed her out the door. This was not how this was supposed to go. Tessa had seen Ryley. If Tessa didn't get eaten by a creepy-crawly stalking the graveyard, she was totally going to haunt Ryley.

This wasn't the first time Ryley had been kicked out of a funeral, but even still, it stung. She was just trying to do the right thing. She glanced over her shoulder and flexed her fingers in an attempt to calm down.

"Maybe I should just quit. Let all these people get haunted. That would teach them." She huffed out an angry breath and tilted her head from side to side, fighting the new rising tension. Henry should have stuck up for her.

Henry wasn't her enemy.

Pastor Peterson now occupied that role.

Things could get out of hand if Ryley was banned from Pastor Peterson's funeral proceedings. Apparently, being a funeral crasher was frowned upon. She'd need to find a way to access the deceased he presided over. What the hell would she do if Peterson told the other religious leaders to ban her as well?

If it happened again, they might get a first-hand peek at the horns holding up her halo.

This was going to require a new tactic in the future, one less stressful. Maybe if Ryley could find a way to get access to the bodies before the funerals, that might save some frustration. Maybe if she had a friend on the inside, or hell, maybe she could convince the funeral home owners to sell her their businesses. Then she could come and go as she pleased.

Wishful thinking. She opened her car door and tossed her purse inside.

The quiet parking lot had one worker headed toward the mortuary.

Pete Roth was the mortuary beautician's

assistant. The young man with dark spiky hair was crossing the parking lot. Her anger dwindled, taking a backseat to the fear slithering down her spine. To the untrained eye, Pete looked like a normal guy, albeit a bit of a nerdy Goth. Ryley wasn't concerned about the guy in general, just the dark evil cloud pulsating like a living breathing threat following him around.

"Has it gotten bigger?" she whispered to herself, unable to take her gaze off the anomaly.

She made a mental note to deal with that cloud of evil soon before it got even more out of control.

Flashing red and blue lights filled the parking lot as a police car pulled in and screeched to a halt.

Her mouth parted, and her eyes widened. Had these people really called the law on her? Ryley folded her arms over her chest. "This should be interesting."

A uniformed officer stepped out. His determined gaze was intent on the chapel.

Henry paused as he stepped out of the chapel doors. A confused look clouded his eyes as he looked at the cop and then at her. He frowned as he jogged down the steps, headed in her direction.

The cop glanced over his shoulder, pausing mid-stride.

Surely, he wasn't there for her. Cops didn't typically respond that fast. At least not to a funeral. She knew firsthand.

And as far as her other transgressions went, they were still dead and buried in the past.

She hoped.

Henry stopped in front of her and rested his hand on her arm. "I'm sorry they treated you like that. If it's any consolation, I told them you were harmless."

"That was a lie." She gestured to the man in uniform. "And I guess they didn't believe you anyway."

Henry glanced over his shoulder. "I doubt he's here for you. He hasn't even reached for his gun or his Taser yet." Henry grinned. "But don't worry. I'll tell him you're my date and I was a witness that you didn't break any laws."

Her lips thinned with irritation as she lifted her chin. This was happening. Her feet refused to move, to run, to leave. It was as though the aggravation and defiance had frozen her in place. Had fate finally caught up to her?

The cop headed in her direction with long, purposeful strides.

"Ms. St. James?" he asked.

"What's the problem, Officer?" Henry asked.

"You're Ms. Ryley St. James, correct?" he asked, ignoring Henry. The cop held up his phone with a picture of her face to compare.

"Yes." She lifted her chin in defiance.

"I'm going to need you to come with me," he said, gesturing to his car.

"Why?" she asked. "I haven't done anything wrong." Her voice got louder.

If she was going down, she was going down fighting. Her heart pounded quickly in her chest.

"What's this about?" Henry asked.

"Tucker St. James."

"My brother?" Fear like no other clogged her veins. She'd spoken with him just that morning. He was headed to court in a case important to both of them. She'd called to wish him luck and was supposed to meet him at the office before he left. How much trouble could he have gotten into in that short of a time span?

"If you'll just come with me, please. Your presence is required." He gestured again toward his cruiser.

"Required?" she asked.

"Yes. We need to leave now."

Tucker's name was the only thing other than the

rattle of handcuffs that could get her to comply. She gave a disappointed glance toward the chapel. Tessa was lingering and watching from just outside the door, confirming that eye contact had indeed been made. Tessa was on to her.

There was no denying that she could see the dead girl. No way to play it off.

A quick thought crossed her mind as she debated the merits of running back into the chapel to send the girl into the light. She had one shot, needing both the dead body and the spirit in the same room. This was it. The body was about to be buried six feet in the ground.

If Ryley was already going to jail, the attempt would be worth it to stop the teen from haunting her the rest of her life.

The cop rested his hand on her elbow, leading her to the cruiser and stealing any chance she might have had to get the job done. He opened the passenger side door and ushered her inside.

Ryley had barely snapped her seat buckle in place when the patrol car raced out of the parking lot, sending a spray of gravel and dirt behind them in its haste.

Goosebumps rose on Ryley's arms just as a

movement from the backseat fluttered in Ryley's peripheral vision and made her turn.

Tessa was staring at her without saying a word.

Ryley shook her head and turned back around, watching the scenery out the window. Thankfully, Tessa wasn't in the mood to talk.

Ryley sitting in the front seat was abnormal, to say the least. The times she'd broken the law before, her typical ride consisted of handcuffs in the backseat.

"Is Tucker okay? He's not hurt, is he?"

Surely, he couldn't have gotten into that much trouble going into work before court. As a defense attorney dealing with criminals, he knew better than most how to protect himself. They'd both had to learn that lesson growing up.

His current client was a wrongfully convicted man. Tucker was no threat to the guy.

The cop ignored her, not even a glance in her direction.

Now that just would not do. It seemed no one had warned this newbie how annoying Ryley could be.

"Where is my brother?" Ryley demanded.

The young officer pressed down on the gas pedal,

speeding up as his grip tightened on the steering wheel.

"Tell me where Tucker is."

No reply.

"If you don't, I'm calling the news station to tell them you kidnapped me and that you're taking me to the woods to shut me up and kill me."

His brows dipped as he finally glanced her way. The officer swallowed hard. "Relax, Ms. St. James. Your brother was fine the last time I saw him at the station. Everything will be explained when I get you there."

Ryley turned her gaze to the scenery flying past.

"You drew the short stick, didn't you?" she asked, turning a darkening gaze on the uniformed punk.

He hesitantly glanced in her direction. "Why would you say that?"

"No one warned you about me?" she asked.

His brows furrowed. "My assignment was to pick you up and deliver you to the precinct."

Now she was getting somewhere. "The only reason I left with you was because you said my brother's name. So, are you telling me that he's been arrested?"

"Not yet," the cop mumbled beneath his breath.

"What the hell does that mean?" she growled,

pulling out her phone. She began Googling the number for the news station. "You have ten seconds to tell me before I call the reporters."

"Judge Jim Henley is a hard judge. There is no gray area with that guy. You're either right or wrong, and he loves to throw people in jail. When I left, your brother was fine. I don't know what state he'll be in when I return."

Perfect. What had Tuck got himself into?

She dialed her brother's number. It went straight to voice mail. She hung up and texted him next, and didn't get a reply.

Her gut tightened at the lack of answers.

The cop glanced at her as if feeling anxiety. "You better not be calling the reporters." He shook his head. "I'm going to be in deep trouble if you do."

She ignored him as effectively as he'd ignored her.

She dialed her brother's office. His assistant, Janet, answered on the second ring.

"Janet, this is Ryley. Let me talk to Tuck."

"He's not here. He went to the police station this morning," she was quick to reply, almost sounding rattled.

"When do you expect him back?"

"An hour ago. Ryley, he's going to be late for

court on the Jennings case. And we both know that your brother would never miss his day in court on that case."

She did know. Ryley had been the one to help her brother find evidence that would get Jennings out of jail and point the investigation toward a real killer. That case hit a little too close to home for both of them.

"No, this case is important to him," she agreed.

"I'm sorry. I have to go and brief one of the partners in the event that Tucker doesn't get back in time."

"Sure. If Tuck shows up, can you have him call me?"

"Of course." Janet hung up on Ryley for the first time ever.

"Okay, so what gives? My brother is at the police station, and I'm getting an escort without shackles? You're going to have to give me something or the next call is to one of my contacts at the news station."

"I don't know the details. I was just told to pick you up and bring you in."

"And if I didn't comply?" she asked.

"In the case you resisted, I was told to put you in

cuffs. Listen, I don't know you, but what I do know is that you're needed at the police department."

Ryley dialed Oscar's number.

Thanks to Wilson's fortune, she'd inherited Oscar's employment, the dead man's dog, and a farm where she could hide out from her father, who wanted her dead. Her daddy would never believe her capable of being such a doer of good deeds, considering she'd tried to kill him before—and missed.

Ryley palmed the pendant against her skin—the bullet casing her father had recently left on her dresser after finding her again. A constant reminder of her own personal danger, which was never far from her thoughts.

Oscar picked up on the first ring. "Did you move the teen along?"

Oscar was a man who could get stuff done for whatever she needed, regardless of the legality. Right now, she was thinking of breaking at least ten different laws.

"Not quite. Listen, I was picked up by the police."

"Say no more. I'll meet you at the police station to bail you out."

"Bring enough bail to cover Tucker, too."

4

"What did you two do?" Oscar asked.

"I'm not sure yet. My presence is being commanded, with or without cuffs," she said, emphasizing the words.

"I'm walking out the door now. I'll make some calls on the way and find out more."

"Thanks, Oscar," she said, disconnecting the call.

She should have told him to bring supplies to move Tessa along and out of the backseat. The ghostly teen was a problem for another day.

It didn't matter if she had her supplies. Sage and salt would be useless to get her and Tucker out of whatever mess they'd created.

Her chest tightened as they pulled into sheriff department's parking lot.

Her fingers hovered over the seatbelt latch as the cop parked. The lot was surprisingly empty other than a few cruisers, her brother's car, and a more expensive Mercedes coupe.

He threw the car into park, and she unbuckled, hesitantly stepping out.

Authority figures gave her hives.

"Let's get you inside," the cop said, rounding the car and ushering her up the stairs and in the door. A swipe of his security ID badge and they were inside the bullpen.

Officers sat entrenched at their desks behind cubical walls. Keyboard clicked, radios squawked, and filing cabinet doors slammed shut as she was ushered through the area. None of the officers offered them a second look as her footsteps echoed down the tiled hall.

Passing the sheriff's office, she spotted Detective Jake Crews and her brother, Tucker, sitting inside behind closed doors.

Neither one noticed her through the blinds as she passed, or even looked in her direction as she was whisked into an interrogation room on the other side of the hall.

"Someone will be with you in just a few minutes," the cop reassured her.

The walls seemed closer than the last time she'd been there. A weird sense of claustrophobia closed in on her. She took a deep, calming breath. Tucker was in the building. She wasn't alone.

Minutes ticked by, and she glanced at her watch, agitated that no one was telling her what the hell was going on. Just as she was about to open the door and demand answers, a man, wearing a tailored black suit fit to perfection, walked in. The elderly ghostly woman following him was wearing a ballgown.

That was unexpected.

Ryley averted her gaze, not wanting to make eye contact with this apparition too.

"I'm FBI Special Agent Roger Keller."

His blond hair was styled as if he had stepped out of a magazine. His high cheekbones and natural tan made him handsome in a silver-spoon, pretty-boy kind of way.

Too pretty for her.

If she had to guess, she'd say he was upper class. Probably came from an upstanding family, judging by the expensive jewels the elderly ghost kept touching around her neck.

She hovered behind the FBI Agent like a lost puppy.

"They never introduce me. Back in my day, it would be considered rude, but I'm Ada Mae Keller of the Manhattan Kellers, and, young lady, I must say, I've met many frauds in my day. Many that claim to see ghosts that wouldn't know a spirit from their own shadow, but that's not you, is it? You can see. You're the real deal." The ghostly woman touched the emerald earrings that matched her necklace.

Bet they would fetch a pretty penny on the black market. Would the old lady tell Ryley her address and the combination to her safe?

She ignored the elderly woman and turned her gaze to Agent Keller. "You got me here. Now what could the feds possibly want with me and my brother?"

Keller folded his arms across his chest. "I'll be the one asking questions."

She raised a brow. If her brother hadn't been sitting in the sheriff's office, she might have just walked out or lawyered up.

"Fine. Am I being charged with something?"

"Not yet," he said with a frown. "Have a seat."

"I'd rather stand. I've been sitting all morning."

"Suit yourself." He tossed a file down onto the desk. "Sorry, I don't have time for pleasantries, Ms. St. James."

Ryley frowned. "You don't strike me as the kind of guy that would care about pleasantries."

"Of course, he would, dear. He was raised with better manners than that, child, and he'd look a lot more presentable if he found his missing cuff link. It fell inside his spare dress shoes in his hurry to pack." Ada Mae sighed.

The ghost was delusional. This guy had the manners of a mosquito looking for sustenance, out for blood and uncaring about the donor. Ryley glanced at the jacket cuffs and held in her grin.

Keller shrugged as if Ryley had been correct in her assessment, even if Ada Mae disagreed. "Yes, well, pleasantries aside, let's get down to business."

"And what business would that be? You know, I own a bar and I've got a liquor license. You look like you could use a nice stiff drink to unruffle your feathers. If you'd care to take this conversation to my establishment?"

The door opened, and another man dressed in a suit stepped inside. He had a natural air of authority about him and gave off a no-nonsense demeanor even though he only seemed to be in his mid to late forties. Regardless of age, if she had to guess, she'd think that this was the judge she'd been warned to watch out for.

"Is this her?" he asked.

"Yes, sir," Keller answered.

"What have you told her?"

"We haven't gotten to the pillow talk yet. I was working on it." Ryley answered for Keller, taking a seat. Her morning was getting longer by the minute.

"Young ladies aren't supposed to mention pillow talk, dear. That's private. Didn't your mother ever teach you that?"

It was obvious this dead lady and Stretch would never be BFF's. They were from two totally different lifestyles.

"So far, she's proved she's outspoken. I've also been told she's going to be a pain in the ass. I can see that they weren't lying," Keller said.

Keller and Ada Mae had their brows raised in disapproval as if it were a family trait.

"Aw, you embarrass me. Which one of these guys do I have to thank for that?"

Neither answered.

"Well, now that everyone knows who I am, please feel free to tell me why I was forced to come here against my will."

"Leave us," the new suit ordered.

"But, Judge, I think you should let me handle this," Keller said with a frown.

Was he handling things? She was no closer to knowing why she was there.

"Keller. I need to talk to Ms. St. James alone, but don't worry. If I have my way, then you two will be spending plenty of time together."

Not likely. Ryley bit her tongue and frowned.

The fine lines around Keller's green eyes deepened. Another family trait. With a single nod of acknowledgment, he left and shut the door behind him.

Impressive. She needed to learn that trick of making cops disappear.

The judge glanced up at the camera, where a red light was shining, before turning his gaze to the two-way mirror. He made a cutting motion on his neck, and the camera blinked out.

No witnesses. That did not bode well for one of them.

5

He turned to her and crossed his arms over his chest. "Do you know who I am?"

"Judge Henley, if I had to guess."

"Did a ghost tell you my name?"

"The fed just called you judge, and the cop that picked me up mentioned your name." She shook her head. "The only spirit that was in here just floated out the door."

Henley glanced to the door. His eyes hardened in an unspoken reprimand. She bet he'd had years to master that.

"As a judge, I've seen my fair share of crime and criminals, both of which I understand. I excel at seeing the truth through the tangled web of lies.

What I don't believe in and have never seen are ghosts."

"Neither have a lot of people," she said. "Is that why I'm here?"

"You think you're special?" he asked.

"The jury's still out, but my momma used to tell me I am. I'm not sure I agree. She was a bad judge of character. She married my dad," Ryley answered honestly.

"I've heard reports that you're gifted. I've also heard that you've helped your brother and Detective Crews on occasion."

"You must have a problem that defies logic. One you can't solve. That's the only reason I get pulled into crap like this with people like you."

"People like me?"

"The kind of person with power who could fix most problems with money. I'm guessing that whatever your problem is, the solution can't be bought."

"You'd be surprised at what I can buy," the judge grumbled under his breath. He pulled out a chair on the other side of the table and took a seat.

Him getting comfortable did not bode well for her getting out of there anytime soon.

"My fiancée is in real estate."

Ryley clasped her fingers together but held in her

audible sigh of relief. They were getting somewhere now. This wasn't the first time she'd helped exorcise ghosts from a house, even if it was the first time a judge was using the weight of his power to force her to help.

"Let me guess. She bought a haunted house?"

"The mansion is in both of our names. We're planning on a remodel. It was supposed to be an easy flip, and then after the first two contractors ran off claiming some nonsense of demons or ghosts scared them off, she was determined to prove them wrong."

Ryley pressed her lips, waiting for the other shoe to fall. Had the fiancée got scared too?

"The first night, she claimed there were noises. The second night, she came home with unexplainable bruises that she got in the middle of the night."

"And she went back?" Ryley couldn't help but ask. She couldn't fix stupid, if that was why she was being held hostage.

"Oh yes, she did. The third night, she put up video cameras intent on proving that someone was doing this to us, trying to scare us from the property."

"Criminals. That's where you excel, right?" Ryley asked, unable to bite her tongue. She'd like to see him be the first judge to throw a ghost in jail. "How did that turn out?"

"When she didn't return home the following morning, I went to check on her. The cameras were pulled down and on the floor. The video feed was filled with snow. Amanda had fallen off one of the balconies. A neighbor had heard her scream and called for help. She's in a coma. Doctors aren't sure if she's going to survive."

"I'm sorry."

His frowned deepened as he watched her.

"If it was a living, breathing criminal, what do you think the motive was? Robbery or just plain psychopathic tendencies?" Ryley asked.

"The money in her purse was still in place, as were all of her cards and license. Her car was still parked outside, and the keys were near where she'd been sleeping. So, it wasn't robbery, and there was no evidence of anyone coming or going from the property, so we haven't determined a motive."

"Sounds like you need a good stakeout, not a medium."

"The police have already searched the property and surrounding area. No one came or went from the house after she arrived. They have searched every inch of that house, looking for clues."

"So, you think a ghost did this to her?"

"I'm not sure what or who did this to her, but I need answers. I don't believe this was an accident, and I don't believe she lost her balance. Something happened to her. Someone pushed her."

Was this a joke? A test? Was this the sheriff's attempt to prove that she was insane or a fraud? If she agreed to help, would they send her to jail or the loony ward? Would he tell her the truth if she asked?

"Why me, and what does any of this have to do with my brother? You sound like you need a priest to come out and bless the house with holy water." She wasn't giving this guy any from her own stolen stash.

"The detective working on the case mentioned your name."

Crews. She had Crews to thank for being in this position. This judge reeked of clout. With a snap of his fingers, he could have her locked up by lunchtime. Judging by the way he watched her, he was still debating his options—put her behind bars or in a white padded cell.

"I'm not a cop. I'm sure there are more qualified people in this building that can help you."

"You do know that your reluctance to help me suggests that you're a con woman."

"You aren't the first to call me that either, although I've never taken money from anyone that I help. I've never run a scam. Life is too short to be worried about looking over my shoulder."

She would know. It was a daily habit she still utilized while watching out for the father that wanted her dead.

"You haven't needed to charge any money. I've read the papers. I know what happened with the Wilson estate. Pity that cousin of his is still holding a grudge."

She'd spent a couple of months in court proceedings having to deal with the cousin's claims, but the last will and testament had held up as uncontestable.

Rocket scientist she was not, but she understood the illegal dynamics this judge was pulling out of his arsenal.

Blackmail. She knew it well. She'd used it before.

"I have a duty to the citizens in town to make sure you don't swindle anyone else. I might even have to go back and look at all of your brother's cases to see which ones you might have tainted."

Tainted. Her eyes narrowed; her body tensed. This was why her bother was here. He wasn't a victim or a criminal; he was leverage.

"Don't hold back now, Judge. You aren't recording this conversation. Let's call this what it is," Ryley poked.

Henley's lips twisted into a smile.

Yep, they were on the same page.

Threats against her brother took things to a whole new level. No witnesses made sense now. No one in their right mind would ever believe that a prestigious, reputable federal judge was issuing threats and blackmailing without proof. It would be his word against hers, and she'd lose that fight.

Still, he had no idea who he was dealing with.

Ryley sat forward and clasped her hands together. "What do you suppose the media is going to think of a judge asking a psychic for help?"

He grinned and tilted his head. "Do you think anyone in this town is going to believe you? I'm sure I'd also win if I sued you for defamation of character."

The judge calmly glanced at his watch as if he had all the time in the world to debate the issue. "Looks like time is of the essence. Your brother and Crews are currently being questioned by the sheriff about the cases you've helped out on. If your brother doesn't leave now, he's going to be late for court on the Jennings case."

"You think you hold all the cards?" she asked, rising from her seat?

"I know I do, Ms. St. James. Now, play nice with Agent Keller and get rid of whatever the hell is in that house. Bring me proof when you're done, and I'll consider forgetting that you live in this town."

"And how am I supposed to prove that a ghost did this when you can't see them?"

"Give me a name or bones or whatever. I need this settled."

He headed for the door and turned at the last minute. "Oh, and, Ms. St. James, you get rid of this son of a bitch, or I promise that it will be your past that comes back to haunt you."

His icy gaze held hers before he walked out and Special Agent Keller walked in.

She stood at the door staring as the judge headed for the sheriff's office. He opened the door without a single knock. Her brother met her gaze, nodded a few times, and hurried out of the office as if the hounds of hell were chasing him. Ryley didn't have to ask where he was headed. He was going to court where an innocent man was counting on him.

Crews' apologetic look just fueled the fire burning through her veins. She stepped back into the room, closed the door behind her, and retook her seat.

"A federal judge is being targeted; that's why the FBI is here," Keller said, folding his arms across his chest.

"Sounds more like the fiancée is the target to me," Ryley countered.

"It's his property too, Ms. St. James."

"Of course." Ryley's foot nervously tapped against the floor; a blackmailing judge getting the upper hand on her was a new twist she'd never considered. "I need the judge's property address."

Keller wrote it down on the back of his card and handed it to her. "We can go do the initial walk-through right now. I'll drive."

"If you don't mind swinging by the cemetery, I'll grab my car and follow you. I've got plans later."

"Why is your car at the cemetery?"

"I was hunting ghosts before I was so rudely carted away."

Keller sighed. "For the record, I don't believe a ghost did this."

"Most cops wouldn't," she said, following him out of the sheriff's department. "And for the record, I'm not sure one did either. The woman might have just lost her balance and tripped."

"Let's go," Keller said, pulling the door open for her and escorting her out the same way she'd entered.

Detective Crews was watching as she passed. A shimmer of regret filled his eyes. He was going to regret it even more when she was done returning the favor.

"Great. Let's hope we can get to the bottom of this before this weekend."

"He has a date, dear. However, she's all wrong for him," Mrs. Ada Mae Keller announced, following behind.

"Apparently, your date this weekend is all wrong for you," Ryley said as Keller opened the door of the SUV.

"Did a ghost tell you that?" Keller asked with a raised brow.

"Actually, Mrs. Ada Mae Keller of the Manhattan Kellers told me that, and she also said that your missing cuff link is in your suitcase tucked in your spare dress shoes. It fell when you were in a hurry to pack." Ryley climbed in. "Do you always bring your mother on your cases?"

He grumbled beneath his breath as he slammed the door and moved around to the driver's side.

Touchy subject. She'd have to remember that. Ryley spotted Oscar walking in her direction.

Keller started the ignition, and she unbuckled her seatbelt. "I'm going to need a minute."

"Husband?" Keller asked.

"No, I'm not married."

Keller grinned. "I know. That's Oscar Rothchild. He's your assistant and lives at the farm with you."

Her mouth parted.

"See, I know things, too. Make it quick. We've got things to do."

She snapped her mouth closed. Perfect. Another man to deal with who thought to rule her life.

Movement in the backseat caught her eye, and Ryley grinned. Tessa from the funeral home was again sitting in the back seat. It was just a matter of time before Tessa demanded help, but this time, Ryley might request a haunting in return, since Stretch wasn't around.

Ryley shut the door while wondering how in the hell she'd gotten stuck working with the FBI, having a judge blackmail her, and having a newly deceased teen haunting her life.

She took another calming breath, which didn't seem to work. Maybe she was in need of more Zen than she thought.

"Looks like you made a new friend." Oscar chuckled.

"The FBI and I are not friends," she said with a frown.

Oscar bent down and glanced in the SUV before commenting. "Then they must have figured out that you're too much to handle. You taking a trip to the federal pen?"

"Not yet, but the day is still early."

"What's the deal? None of my contacts know what the hell is going on. It's not often I'm left in the dark."

"I thought I had an easy schedule today, only helping a spirit to cross and working at the bar tonight. Neither seems to be in my cards. I'm apparently on a new case."

"I thought you weren't doing that anymore, especially with men carrying badges and wearing crew cuts."

"I don't have a choice." She took a picture of the address on the back of the FBI card and texted it to Oscar. "I'll be spending the next few nights at this location. I'm going to need someone to cover for me at the bar."

"You know Kent is going to have a coronary," Oscar said, crossing his arms over his chest.

"Tell him to take it up with Judge Henley." Aggravation seeped from her voice, and she paused, reeling it back in. "I'm sorry. I know it sucks, but it can't be helped; trust me." She nodded. "I have a feeling my life outside the bar is about to get a ton more complicated. We might need to hire more staff."

The SUV window lowered. "Ms. St. James, if you don't mind."

"It appears I'm on the clock." She rolled her eyes. "I'll be home later for a change of clothes and to pick up some supplies, and judging by my escort, I might be bringing the fed with me. You might want to pick up the place and hide any of your illegal activities."

"You don't need to worry about me, but I'll make sure you have clean sheets." Oscar grinned like he was enjoying her predicament a little too much.

"No need. He's not my type."

"Fine, then I'll set an extra plate at the table if you don't run him off first," Oscar said.

"I'm going to give it my best try." She chuckled.

6

The ride to the cemetery was quiet. The parking lot was almost empty. A few stragglers were leaving the area. A familiar ghostly woman, who was always at the cemetery, was sitting in front of the same grave. The wilted flowers needed replaced.

Another spirit like the teen that Ryley had missed.

Keller dropped her off, and she followed him across town out past the warehouse district and the high-rises that dotted the skyline.

Just beyond that was the other part of town, the other side of the tracks, where her kind was never meant to live.

Lavish sprawling houses gave way to less appealing properties. As they drove farther out, the houses weren't as well kept. The grass was a little higher. The shrubs and weeds multiplied, and then the overgrowth of trees came into view, as did another property. This one was different, broken down as if the very core of its soul had lost a fight.

He stopped at a gated fence surrounding the property. The faded mailbox numbers hung askew. The weathered name on the box read Bateman.

The three-story home towered in the distance, blending in with the ancient pine trees. The *Danger* and *No-trespassing* signs attached to the locked fence did little to keep prying eyes and trespassers out. The chain-link fence was pulled back, an easy obstacle for vandals to get past.

The signs were directed toward those that didn't belong. For once, it wasn't her. She didn't have to sneak onto the property to break in.

This time they had a damn key.

The gate creaked open, and she followed Keller's SUV through, parking in front of the run-down building.

Layers of spray-painted words littered the stucco walls, only slightly hidden by vines climbing toward the sky. The dying brown vines never made it past the second floor. Proof that even Mother Nature had a hard time inhabiting the place.

Ryley stared up at vacant and broken windows, wondering who might still be lingering inside.

"Paperwork shows he paid pennies for it," Keller said, walking up beside her.

"This place gives me a bad feeling." She said the words, staring trance-like at the third floor, knowing that someone or something was staring back at her from beyond the broken blinds. What she'd thought would be an easy fix now seemed overwhelming.

"You look scared," Keller said.

"Not scared. I'm being cautious." She dropped her gaze from the third floor to the second-story window, where a ghostly face watched them from behind the cracked window panes.

"If we're going to get this done by Friday, we need to get a move on."

"Always in a rush. You might do well to slow down and rely on your spidey senses, especially in a place like this."

This old place had potential. It was spacious and big enough that even she could have found a use for it and renovated it through her foundation.

Maybe she should tell the judge that there was no hope, no saving it. Maybe she could buy it off of him dirt cheap and use it as a halfway house or orphanage. She bet the neighbors would love her even more. But one truth remained. She needed to move these ghosts along before even that could happen.

Ryley, also known as the new primary donor and decision-maker of the Wilson Foundation, could bankroll the renovations to make this a shelter for battered women or something. There was potential.

Ryley's life was crazy enough with the apparitions she could see. Throw in a town full of people either wanting her help or believing her a fraud, and a father that wanted her dead, and there were few places she could hide off the map and breathe.

Three more spirits on different floors appeared as if getting the message that fresh prey was outside the front door waiting to come in.

The air filled with heated static. Her resolve was stuck in her throat. She'd almost never been scared of the Great Beyond, but something in her gut was telling her to burn this place down.

Evicting ghosts was easier said than done.

Keller's phone rang. "Excuse me. I have to take this."

"You do that. I'm going to get a look inside." She nodded and held her hand out for the key.

"Don't steal anything." He handed it to her and then walked off.

"No promises," she called out as she walked up the cracked concrete stairs onto the wrap-around porch. Using the key, she unlocked the door. It creaked as she shoved it open and then stepped inside.

A shiver skirted her spine as a cold breeze flew past at warp speed. There one minute and gone the next.

That was a warning glance.

One that suggested Ryley St. James wasn't welcome here.

She stood still in the musty, dank space as fear slithered down her spine like a ghost rattling a chain against an attic floor.

On the ground floor, sunlight was blocked by the boarded-up windows, letting only a sliver of light inside between the slats.

Her racing heart pounded in her ears. As many times as she'd done this, it was always the same anticipation.

Her gaze darted around the room. A cot was laid out next to the fireplace, long since extinguished. A blanket lay unfolded on top of a cot. An empty wine glass sat on the floor next to a forgotten book.

Maybe Amanda had gotten drunk and had fallen over the ledge. Ryley was grasping at straws.

She inhaled and walked to the nearest wall, resting her palm on the drywall. She closed her eyes, and a tingle of energy singed her fingertips. A ghost was most certainly lying in wait.

Get out. The dreadful warning flashed in her mind.

She wasn't supposed to be there.

Not in this building.

It didn't matter. She wasn't leaving. Not yet.

She'd been tasked with figuring out who was residing in the space before driving the occupants out. Her brother's career depended on it.

Ryley stepped forward. The old wooden floorboard creaked beneath her feet.

This old house had history. It was in every nook and cranny. Yellow-stained dust-covered sheets lay over the old furniture, protecting it from the damage of time and elements. A musty smell of mold permeated the air, making her stomach queasy.

On one wall, the once-popular and expensive floral wallpaper was peeling and crumbling to the touch. On the other, the wood paneling was coated with centuries of wax buildup.

Nothing was safe in this space.

Creak. Creak. Creak.

Her gaze shot to the stairs. The sound of footsteps from above rattled her resolve.

Restless earth-trapped spirits were hard to help. How they were in life carried over in death. Souls were not all good and not all bad. They'd transition with the demeanors they'd had in life, and most times, theirs and hers clashed.

Whispers carried through the walls.

Every fiber of her being felt smothered. Her chest tightened, making it difficult to breathe. This place held secrets. If she wasn't careful, she'd be just another victim at these ghostly hands.

This place reeked of warnings and ill tidings.

Dulled crystals clinked on the chandelier, drawing her attention to the movement above her head. The once-glorious piece that suggested prestige now hung askew and broken above.

One strong wind would send the light fixture crashing down on Ryley's head as if she were a bullseye. Ryley took a tentative step back.

A creepy black mass slithered on the ceiling above, making her pause. Goosebumps covered her arms.

She'd eased onto the second step when she heard the noise on the landing above again. A residual scream rooted her in place.

"What the hell was that?" Keller asked, drawing

his weapon.

"Nothing you'll be able to shoot," she said as he hurried past her up the stairs to the second floor.

"Stay put," he growled in his haste.

Fear made her vulnerable. Fear put her in jeopardy. The lurking fear would never strangle her vocal cords.

These ghosts would not win.

With the windows boarded up, she moved to the doorway and confirmed her suspicions. Both Ada Mae Keller and Tessa were standing beyond the gate, out in the road as if there was some type of barrier keeping good spirits out, or maybe the barrier was to keep the bad spirits in.

Something wasn't just wrong with this house. Something was seriously wrong.

Several minutes later, Keller reappeared at the top of the stairs. "There's not a single soul here."

That was a lie. There was more than one. Spirits weren't just inside the house; they were outside too. "None you can see. You might want to cancel your date."

He frowned. "Why is that?"

"This isn't what I would call a typical haunting."

"No? Then what would you call it?"

"An infestation."

7

"You're sure?" he asked.

"As sure as I am that Ada Mae is from the Manhattan Kellers," Ryley said, handing him the key. "You know, I can handle this. You don't have to stay."

"Yes, I do. This is a federal investigation."

Her lips twitched. "I'd love to read that report when you get done with it."

"I'm sure you would."

"What kind of reprimand is in your file to get assigned this case?"

He didn't answer, piquing her interest.

"Fine, keep your secrets for now. Still, there's not much you'll be able to do here. You can't see them. You can't shoot them or throw them in jail. You won't even be able to protect me, much less yourself.

You're just going to get in the way. Your gun and badge don't scare anyone in the afterlife, and actually, if the head entity is as bad as I think he might be, you might just antagonize him."

"That should be helpful, right?" His gaze studied the room with intense curiosity. He really believed he could help. "I'm not leaving, Ms. St. James."

"My name is Ryley. Mrs. St. James was my mother. Listen, I need to run and get more supplies and handle some things. I'll meet you back here tonight for our sleepover."

His expression stilled and grew serious. "That's not how this is going to work."

"No?" She sighed, weary of the impending argument.

"Consider me your shadow. Judge Henley wants to make sure you don't stage any of this."

Her brows furrowed. "What would I have to gain by doing that? I didn't even know Henley before today, and I haven't met his fiancée."

"Actually, you knew her years ago, only you knew her as Amanda Greenly. She's your brother's ex-girlfriend."

Memories of Tucker's ex-girlfriend flooded her mind. The girl who broke his heart, Amanda had dated Tucker all through high school and two years of college before she dumped him and broke things off. She'd been the love of his life.

The situation was becoming clearer. The reason Ryley got dragged into this was starting to make sense. Was this some sort of payback? It probably was if Henley was remotely aware Ryley and Amanda had history. None of it was good. Not after what she'd done to Tucker.

Ryley had a motive, and worse than that, Tuck might have had a motive, too.

"She dumped my brother for another guy. She claimed Tuck wasn't the right man for her. So, I'm guessing Judge Henley was the guy she was screwing around with. That would explain his interest in my abilities and the desire to screw with my family."

Keller remained quiet, as if letting Ryley figure out the puzzle pieces and how they all fit together. His lack of input was an answer in and of itself.

She slowly nodded, hating Henley more and more each minute. First, he'd stolen Tuck's girlfriend and now demanded Ryley's help by threatening Tucker's career.

Maybe she should leave the house infestation. Maybe it would serve him right. Although paybacks would be much worse. If she was going to send these ghosts packing, maybe she'd give them Henley's current address.

She could get them out of this house and moved to a new place. She would have completed the mission. Win/win…well, for everyone but Henley and Amanda.

Maybe she'd just send Stretch instead. Less fuss.

"Fine. Follow me around. Make sure I'm not hiding a sound machine in the walls, but if you're going to be my shadow, you might as well help." An evil grin slid across Ryley's face as she headed back to the door, waiting for Keller to lock up. Not that anyone in their right mind would bother to venture inside.

The minute she drove out the gate again, the heaviness on her chest eased and the dizziness subsided. There was much more going on at that property than anyone knew.

Ada Mae disappeared inside Keller's SUV while Tessa appeared again in Ryley's backseat.

"Why were you at my funeral? I don't know you," Tessa said as Ryley headed across town to the farm.

"You shouldn't be here. You need to go into the light where the people that love you are waiting," Ryley said, glancing once in the rearview mirror.

"You can see me and hear me." Tessa's eyes widened

before she disappeared and reappeared in the passenger seat, hopping around like a jumping bean.

"Yes. Now listen. I've got a lot on my plate. Just tell me what your unfinished business is, and I'll see if I can help after I deal with Henley's house issue."

Tessa frowned. A momentary sadness filled her face before it flashed in anger. "I shouldn't be dead."

Okay then. Ryley was sure that this teen had moved past the denial stage.

"But you are. You got the shaft and didn't get a do-over like some of those other near-death-experiencers. So just tell me who you want to say goodbye to, and then you can be on your way to a better place."

Tessa's brows furrowed. "I'm going to kill him."

"I'm pretty sure that's not going to get you"—Tessa vanished before Ryley finished—"into the light."

It was just as well. Fingers crossed, Tessa was gone for good, but even when spirits figured out about Ryley's abilities, they never stayed gone for long. She was the last connection to the living for most of them.

The seat had been vacated only a mere second when Stretch appeared in the vacated seat.

"The dearly departed must really like car rides.

One pops in just about every time I get behind the wheel," Ryley noted.

"Don't be ridiculous. You're just less preoccupied while driving alone," Stretch answered.

"Maybe I should start listening to the radio or drive with the window down. I'd be less approachable."

"They'd just appear in front of your car so that you hit them. That way they get you to stop."

True. Ghosts always figured out how to get her attention.

"Well, nice of you to join me." Ryley glanced in the ghost's direction. "You didn't stick around at the chapel today, and you disappeared last night. I'm beginning to think that you have more important things to do."

Stretch grinned. *"I thought you were going to see your brother after the funeral, but instead, you went to the police station, and there is no way in hell that I'm step-ping foot back in one of those places of my own free will."*

"Fine, at least tell me that you didn't go watch another booty call last night."

"I might have when I realized you weren't getting any."

"You still could have stuck around to help me

identify that black clouded mass following that Pete guy around."

"Oh, I can't go near that. I don't know what it is. I just know it's dangerous."

"And here I thought nothing scared you."

"And here I thought I'd never see you willingly helping the police again, and it looks like you've graduated to the FBI," Stretch said, peering out the back window. *"Well, at least he's a cute one. You could have done worse."*

"Cute or not, he's a pain in my ass." Ryley glanced in the rearview mirror to see if Keller had blown through the last red light or if she'd managed to lose him yet. "But in all seriousness, I wouldn't be helping him if I wasn't being blackmailed."

Ryley's ancestral line was caked with lawbreakers just like the mud and Bondo stuck on Oscar's truck. The fact she was helping and not sitting in a jail cell after refusing made her realize she hadn't just fallen from the tree; she'd rolled a mile away from those roots. Still, no amount of distance could undo the little bit of her rotten core she coveted.

Just as quickly as Stretch had appeared, she vanished. She'd once told Ryley that being around cops that she wasn't having sex with made her cranky. A habit that Ryley must have picked up.

Ryley pulled into the farm and parked, waiting for Keller to do the same.

"Nice place," he said, glancing around the area. "I wouldn't have guessed you're a country girl."

She held in her grin. She was counting on her dad to believe the same thing.

"This was Old Man Wilson's place. I'm sure Henley filled you in."

"Yeah, the weird rich guy that left everything to whoever attended his funeral. Lucky you."

And then some. The door opened as she neared, and Oscar stood at the threshold. Ringwald came bounding out the door, and Ryley braced for impact.

The guard dog greeted her with a vengeance every time she'd come home, since the very first time she'd fed him a steak.

He'd barely reached her before he was standing on his back legs, trying with all his might to lick her face.

"Who's this cute guy?" Keller asked, reaching out to pet him.

Ringwald snapped at the hand, dropping to the ground and stepping between Ryley and Keller. A low growl emitted through this body.

"Good dog." Ryley grinned. "He's a guard dog and doesn't like men."

"Now that's not true." A familiar voice came from the house as private eye Logan Bane stepped out onto the porch. "Ringwald likes me just fine."

The tension in Ryley's shoulders eased. Bane was a lawbreaker like Ryley. He sometimes crossed the line to get the job done. The fact that he was out at the farm meant Oscar was already getting some behind-the-scenes help.

"You lost?" she asked with a grin as she headed into the house.

"I heard you were making new friends. I didn't believe it, so I had to come to see for myself," Bane said, following behind her into the kitchen. "I guess it's true."

Keller held out his hand. "I'm—"

"FBI Special Agent Roger Keller," Bane answered for him. "Nice to finally meet you. I'm private investigator Logan Bane."

"You've been busy." She glanced at Oscar with an unspoken appreciation.

"Well, someone has to look out for your best interests." Oscar grabbed the coffee pot and took more cups out of the cupboard as if to offer their guests a mug.

She'd missed that etiquette class.

The three talked in easy banter as Ryley walked back through the house to the front door.

Ada Mae remained on the porch, trying to cross the salt-lined barrier.

"He's in excellent hands. Don't worry. I'll return him in one piece. Maybe." Ryley grinned at the old ghostly lady.

Ada Mae's mouth parted, and she gasped, reaching for her jewels as Ryley shut the door in the ghostly woman's face.

"Who were you talking to?" Keller was standing behind her, watching her with his sharp, questioning gaze.

"Your mom. Ada Mae."

"Ada Mae was my grandmother, not my mom."

"Why didn't you correct me before?" She gawked.

"You didn't ask. You just assumed."

"Yeah, well, I'm going to need the number to her Botox doctor." Ryley grinned.

"It's not Botox. It's in my genes."

"I'm sure it is." Ryley winked in passing as she headed up the stairs. When Keller started to follow, she blocked his path. "As pretty as your genes are, I'm just going to go change. Oscar and Bane will keep you company."

Keller's phone rang again.

"You need me to show you how to turn your phone on vibrate?"

"No," Keller growled and stepped off the stairs, answering as he stepping into the living room.

She shrugged and met Oscar's gaze. "I'm just going to change. Can you offer him a drink, or better yet, don't? Maybe it's not wise to feed the strays. They may feel comfortable to visit again."

"You do know how to please," Oscar said as Bane walked out of the kitchen.

Bane chuckled in passing with a wave of his hand. "I can see that you're no worse for wear from your time at the police station."

"Thanks for stopping by," she called out.

"You'll be seeing me again." He wiggled his fingers in passing and glanced in the direction of the living room where Keller was on the phone. "Try to stay out of jail."

"I don't think it's in my DNA," she said, heading up the stairs.

Oscar chuckled as Ryley went to her room and changed. After grabbing a backpack and shoving some of her things inside of it, she headed back toward the kitchen to find Oscar offering Keller a brownie. She grabbed one from the plate in passing and tossed her backpack onto the counter, digging around in the pantry.

"Do you care to explain all the details now?" Oscar asked as Keller took a seat.

"I figured you already knew, since Bane was here," she said.

"He's doing some research for me," Oscar said.

"I bet he is." Ryley shoved the cereal boxes out of the way and kept looking. "Judge Henley is blackmailing me into fixing his ghost problem."

Keller choked on his brownie, and Oscar poured him a cup of coffee.

"You're lying," Keller said, wiping at his watering eyes.

"Maybe about other things, but not about this. Trust me. I wouldn't be helping Henley unless he was blackmailing me," Ryley said, trying unsuccessfully to catch her brownie crumbs in her hand.

"That's true. Ryley refuses to work with law enforcement of any kind unless she's personally invested."

Oscar grabbed a napkin and handed it to Ryley. "Tell me what you're looking for before you get crumbs everywhere and destroy the organized pantry."

"Salt," she answered.

"Your bag of salt is in your trunk."

"That little bag isn't going to do the job. I'm going to need more, a lot more."

Oscar moved her out of the way and pulled out a large five-gallon container, hefting it over to the table. He popped open the lid and grabbed a measuring cup. "How much will you need?"

She took the measuring cup, dumped it inside the bin, and closed it back up. Easing all fifty pounds back down to the floor, she struggled to slide it out into the hallway to sit by the door.

Oscar tilted his head as he watched her. "That bad?"

"Worse. I think."

Oscar frowned. "I wouldn't have guessed that. The property at the address you gave me has been owned by a single family."

"Maybe the entire family were serial killers."

"Only one family has lived on the property?" Keller asked. "How do you know that?"

Oscar gestured down the hall. "It's my job to know everything that involves Ryley."

"Did you think I keep Oscar around because he's just a pretty face? He's in charge of the sound machines we hide in the walls. Keep up, Keller." Ryley chuckled, following Oscar into the library.

The tripod easels that Oscar used for Old Man Wilson's research years ago had been upgraded to computerized smart boards.

A picture of the Bateman house was on the screen, along with several computerized documents of deeds.

Family portraits that looked as though they dated back three or four generations were below the paperwork.

She recognized one of the faces immediately. The one that had been staring at her from the second-story window.

"You've been busy," Ryley said in passing to get a better look.

"I had help," Oscar announced.

Bane. This was why Bane had made a trip to the farm.

"Who are they?" Ryley asked.

"Captain Archibald Bateman bought the land a century ago and built a house on it. The property has been passed down for generations," Oscar said, meeting her at the board. He opened the file containing even more pictures. "This was the original house."

It looked nothing like the one that they'd just been inside. It was a plain and simple construction.

A man was dressed in a suit with a pipe hanging out of his mouth. His tan skin suggested he spent a lot of time out in the sun. A woman in a long dress stood in front of the porch, along with ten children. "That house isn't the one still standing."

In the next picture, the same family was standing in front of a boat with a sign in the background that read *Bateman's Charter Service*.

"No, the Batemans have rebuilt through the years." He pulled up several more pictures of different-styled houses until the recent one. "All the Batemans were prominent businessmen in town."

"What else did you find out about the property?"

"Nothing but tragedy has taken place on that property. The first house burned to the ground. One family member died. The second house was struck by lightning. The third had a freak tornado come through that tore it down. Each generation has had to rebuild. The one that is still standing belonged to Gerald Bateman. The last owner. He and his wife couldn't have any children, so they turned to adoption. A boy and a girl, although I can't find anything that tells me what happened to the children. I'm still searching."

She moved closer to the pictures, memorizing

each of the family faces that Oscar and Bane had uncovered.

"Are they buried on the property?" Keller asked.

"That was my first thought, so I started digging into it. The last three generations of family members are all buried in the older section of Glendale Cemetery. I haven't had time to look back any further than that."

"Find out what you can," Ryley said, moving down the sea of faces. "Only a couple of these people are still haunting the place. All the other ghosts I saw aren't in these pictures."

"I'll keep digging."

"Thanks, Oscar." She patted his back and grabbed her backpack again, heading for the front door.

Oscar followed. "How did it go at the funeral?"

Ryley turned back to him, trying as she might to keep her answer socially acceptable for the FBI agent. "It didn't. I never got to say goodbye. A uniform picked me up before I made it to the casket."

Oscar frowned. His gaze landed on the salt line at the door. "A problem for another day?"

"Aren't they all?" She let out a heavy sigh and gestured for Keller to grab the container of salt to carry to her car.

"I'll call you if I find out more," Oscar offered.

"Thanks." She turned at the last minute. "Oh, and it might be wise to keep emergency service personnel on standby just in case one of us falls off the balcony too."

"I always do with you," Oscar said.

8

Keller loaded the tub of salt into the back of his SUV and then took her backpack and other things and tossed those inside, too. "We should stick together. What else do you need?"

She popped her trunk and grabbed her sleeping bag and go-bag filled with additional sage and protections that she'd spent years collecting and making. She handed that to him, too, before climbing into the passenger seat. "I don't suppose you have a demonologist on speed dial?"

"Afraid not." His courteous voice was patronizing.

She shrugged and shut the passenger door. "I guess this is as good as it gets."

A chill swept through the SUV. Goosebumps rose on Ryley's arms. They had incoming.

Tessa Murphy appeared in the back seat, and Ryley let out a tired sigh. "What is it going to take to move you along?"

"I need you to talk to my sister. Explain things."

"Fine. Tell me what you want and then leave. I've got more pressing issues to deal with."

The ghost stubbornly shook her head. *"No. You talk to her first, and then I'll leave."*

Keller climbed into the SUV and started the ignition. "How about we get something to eat and hit my hotel to grab a few things before we go get settled in for the night?"

Ryley glanced in the backseat, and Tessa leaned forward, trying to touch Keller's arm. He shivered in response.

"Sure, but I have a stop to make and one more thing to deal with first."

"Okay, what's the address?"

Ryley turned in her seat with a raise of her brow.

Tessa gleamed as though she'd hit the lottery.

"She's at 1527 Wilmington."

Ryley repeated the address and hoped for a better outcome than what had happened at the funeral home.

She would have lost that bet.

Keller glanced in the backseat with a frown. "Who are you talking to?"

"A temporary complication," Ryley answered as she righted herself in the seat.

* * *

Through the open curtains at 1527 Wilmington, people dressed in black lingered inside the home and groups gathered in the yard.

"I thought you said your sister lives here," Ryley growled.

"Your complication is a mission for a dead person?" Keller asked.

Ryley ignored his questions.

"This is my parents' house. She's here."

Through the open window, there was a face Ryley recognized. Henry was talking to a woman. They leaned into each other as if talking in hushed tones until another man walked over.

The woman looked away as the newcomer laid a kiss on her cheek. Henry exchanged a handshake with the man.

Ryley pulled out her phone. Maybe this wouldn't

be as hard as she thought, not with someone on the inside.

She held in her grin and called Oscar to find Henry's cell number.

Within a couple of minutes, her phone dinged with the digits.

Ryley crafted the text and hit Send. *We need to talk.*

Henry checked his phone and then re-pocketed it.

He probably had no idea who the message was from. She would have ignored it, too.

Normal people wouldn't have bothered him at a time like this. Normal people would have tried again later. She wasn't normal.

Spam time.

This is Ryley St. James. Ignore me again and I might just come inside to find out who the woman is. I'm pretty sure it's really illegal for you to be in the middle of an affair.

Send.

Need me to flirt with her boyfriend, or is that her husband? I can be a distraction to give you more time to talk in hushed tones.

Send.

It's been a while for you, hasn't it? Do you need lessons? Rule number 1 is to find a dark corner.

Send.

Or, better yet, a room with a door.

Send.

Need me to refresh your memory on what happens when you get her alone?

Send.

I can do this all day. I'm outside watching.

Send.

She lifted her gaze to the window again.

Henry sighed and pulled out his phone, looking at the screen again, scrolling before his gaze shot to the window. He took a step closer to the window and scanned his surroundings until he found her.

"Boyfriend?" Keller asked.

"No, just an acquaintance I like to annoy."

"What are we doing here? Tell me you aren't going inside to give them a message from their recently deceased loved one."

"Of course not," she lied as she waved to Henry and climbed out of the SUV with Keller following her.

Henry excused himself and then stepped outside, glancing over his shoulder as he pulled the door shut. He hurried across the lawn to where she waited.

"What are you doing here? Are you trying to upset them even more?"

She didn't answer. It was probably sacrilegious to lie to a man of the cloth. "Unlike you, I actually am a rule-breaker, and I brought a badge with me."

Henry glanced up at Keller and frowned. "I'm pretty sure he can't do anything since, technically, you'd be the one trespassing."

"Don't bring me into whatever this is. I can assure you that this isn't a federal matter." Keller held up his hands.

"Listen, I just need to talk to Tessa's sister. If you just point her out, I'll say a few words and then be on my way." Ryley offered up a fake smile for good measure.

Henry glanced over his shoulder. "I don't think that's a good idea."

"The woman you were just talking to is the sister, right?"

"Ryley, we don't have time for this," Keller said, glancing at his watch.

"Listen to your friend," Henry said with a jut of his chin.

Ryley rested her hand on her hip and glanced at

Keller. "You're not helping, and if it wasn't for you guys hauling me to the police station, I could have taken care of this on my own. But nooo…so now you're just going to have to give me a minute."

Keller's face remained stoic, as if she'd hit the required nerve. "Make it fast, and if the girl doesn't want to talk to you, you can't make her."

Henry ran his hand through his hair. "You're not going to let this go, are you?"

"No. I'm not."

Resignation crossed his face, and the tense muscles in his face softened. "If you want to talk to Tessa's sister, you're going to have to do it after she leaves here."

"Fine. You have my number now in your phone. Just text me when and where."

Henry nodded.

The house door opened again, and the noise from inside spilled out into the yard as the Murphys and Pastor Peterson stepped out onto the grass. Marvin was pointing in their direction, and his wife had hold of his arm as if holding him back from a confrontation.

Tessa was hovering near her mother. The sad look on her face made Ryley believe the girl most definitely had some type of unfinished business. Poor kid.

"Please just go," Henry said, pulling open her car door.

Ryley frowned. "Looks like your girlfriend is leaving with another woman and man."

"She's not my girlfriend," Henry said. "She's…a work colleague."

Henry opened the car door.

They came closer toward them and climbed into a car parked two spots away from Ryley, giving her a good glimpse at the woman's and man's faces. The same cheekbones and smile as the ghostly spirit that had been following Ryley around for the last couple of hours. The other woman was Tessa's sister.

"Just let me talk to Tessa's sister for a minute, and I won't ever bother her again." Ryley shut the door.

Henry reopened it and stepped in her way. "Go home. I'll text you later."

"Cause clergymen don't lie."

Sadness clouded Henry's eyes. "I don't lie, Ryley."

Keller waited for her to get into the car and then climbed behind the wheel. Starting the engine, he pulled away from the curb.

She was going to need to deal with Pastor Peterson, and soon. She narrowed her eyes at the pastor in passing.

Just as the thought crossed her mind, Stretch appeared in the back seat as if on cue. *"That man does not like you."*

"I'm thinking you could visit him for the next few nights and give him a new understanding of the holy spirit."

"Who are you talking to now?" Keller asked.

"My spirit guide," Ryley answered with a mischievous grin.

"Maybe. If I can fit you in my schedule." Stretch's smile widened in approval.

Even if she hadn't yet agreed, she would.

"What schedule? You're dead, and if I didn't know any better, I'd think that you had a daily booty call. You seem to disappear around the same time every day."

"Don't I wish, child. Don't I wish," Stretch said, as if remembering times past. *"I guess I have some time now to go rattle some chains."*

"I'm not opposed to you picking the chain with the cross around his neck," Ryley called out as Stretch disappeared.

"I'm going to pretend I didn't just hear you tell a ghost to go haunt a pastor."

"Okay. Pretend away."

Keller pulled up to the stop sign, and she pointed to the right. "Let's eat. Aggravating people makes me famished."

"I'm sure it does." Keller shook his head.

She could already see the headache forming behind his eyes.

Yeah, it was just a matter of time before she ran him off, too. At this rate, he might not even make it through the night.

9

The diner wasn't too terribly busy for the late afternoon rush. The Grease Pit was one of Ryley's favorite places. Not so much because of the atmosphere but because of the food and the fact that one of her favorite locals worked there.

Ryley's friend, Maggie, waitressed to make ends meet during the day, but at night and on weekends, she investigated the paranormal, trying to prove the things that both she and Maggie could see.

Maggie was a medium. She had her own side hustle with a website, only she had a strict policy to give readings only to people that didn't live in town. She'd been burned once before.

Maggie didn't look like her interest was anywhere in the paranormal. Her hair was styled in a coif straight out of the fifties. She looked as though she had a husband and two point five kids waiting at home behind a white picket fence.

Nothing could be further from the truth. The woman's roommate worked at the morgue, and they used a coffin as their living room table.

Ryley slid into her normal booth, pressed against the big glass window with an unobstructed view of the parking lot.

Maggie was quick to the table, although she looked a tad confused at Ryley's new guest.

Those who knew Ryley knew her well enough to know that she didn't take to strangers.

Maggie put the coffee cups in front of them and filled them both. "I wasn't expecting you until later." She glanced at Keller. Her frown deepened. "And I was expecting you with Oscar."

"Maggie, this is Keller. Keller, this is Maggie," Ryley said by way of introduction.

Questions gleamed in Maggie's eyes.

"Don't I know you?" Maggie asked Keller.

His cheeks tinted. "No, but I've been told I have a familiar face."

Maggie pinched her lips together and grabbed her notepad as if still trying to place him in her head. "What can I get you two?"

"Pancakes and bacon for me, and a whole apple pie to go."

"The whole apple pie?" Maggie asked.

"It's going to be a long night."

"Right," Maggie said, glancing at Keller. "And what about you?"

"The same, but without the added apple pie. I'll just eat some of hers."

"You don't know Ryley very well if you think that." Maggie chuckled and walked off.

"I'm going to need a late-night snack. I already warned you that annoying people makes me hungry."

"You won't be around anyone to annoy. You're going to be with me."

Ryley lifted the coffee cup to her lips with a great big grin and took a sip as the FBI agent mentally put the pieces together.

She had that effect on people. He asked questions and prodded for background into Ryley's life the entire time they ate, and she did the same, answering his questions with questions of her own.

It was a stalemate all around. Yet something in her gut was screaming that this guy held deeply rooted secrets. It was in the way he watched their surroundings. Her criminal father had taught her early on how to read people and pay attention. Maybe she needed to probe a little deeper.

Make him just a tad bit more uncomfortable.

They paid their checks and stopped by his hotel room. He went straight to his suitcase and grabbed a change of more comfortable clothes, stuffing it into the FBI-issued backpack. He paused at his shoes and tipped the first one over. Empty. When he tipped the second shoe, the cuff link dropped into his hand.

"I guess you were right," he said as she moved around.

"Ada Mae would be pleased you no longer look like a heathen," Ryley answered.

The bed was untouched. The toiletries were still in the case sitting on the counter next to the sink. His suitcase had been tucked in a corner. A hanging bag hung from the open closet. This might be his hotel room, but there was nothing to suggest he'd been staying there.

"When did you get in town?" she asked from across the room while he was sending a text on his phone.

"A couple of nights ago."

Her gaze shot to his, and she stopped in mid-stride. "But I thought this accident just happened."

"Oh, it did. I was already here on business. It's why I was assigned."

He hit Send and re-pocketed the phone. "You ready?"

"The question is, are you ready, Special Agent Roger Keller?"

"As ready as I'll ever be." Keller slung the backpack over his arm and opened the hotel room door.

As Ryley stepped outside, Tessa was pacing the sidewalk.

"Can't you go hang out with your family or something? I can't talk to your sister until I get a text saying the coast is clear."

Tessa lunged in Ryley's direction. *"You have to warn her before it's too late. You have to tell her to let me go. If she gets caught up in this mess, she's going to get hurt, possibly have an accident just like me."*

Keller walked by. "I don't even want to know who you're talking to now. Just make it quick."

"Tessa, the teen whose funeral you pulled me away from. She's haunting me now," Ryley called out. Keller might not want to know, but it served him right to have to deal with the same aggravating haunting.

Keller hit the fob on the SUV and tossed his things into the trunk.

"You didn't tell me that you were murdered. What were you doing, and who killed you?

"I don't know," Tessa growled before vanishing again.

Ryley shook her head as she stepped over to the SUV where Keller was waiting with the passenger door opened.

"Can't you tell them we have more pressing things to handle? And while you're at it, tell them I'm not a taxi, either." Keller climbed in the other side and glanced in the backseat as if to double-check no one was hiding.

"She was on the sidewalk, and she's already vanished, but your backseat is like a magnet for these ghosts, popping in and out at will. I'm beginning to think your backseat is a portal. You should get that fixed." A teasing laugh slipped free.

Keller's eye twitched as he started the ignition.

"You know, if you don't like being a chauffeur, I can drive my own car. You wouldn't have to worry about ghosts at all."

"If you did that, then who's going to entertain me?"

Entertainment purposes. Keller probably didn't believe in ghosts or the afterlife, not a cop like him.

Maybe she shouldn't antagonize him lest she end up in jail.

She didn't answer. Instead, she fired off a text to Henry. *Now?*

He answered with a two-word reply. *Not yet.*

It's important. I don't think Tessa's car accident was an actual accident.

It went unread. Ryley rubbed at the forming headache.

Clouds formed in the early evening sky. The scent of apple pie permeated the backseat. "We're going to need supplies."

"I thought that's what we've been getting," Keller said.

"Not ghost hunting supplies. We need sleepover supplies like drinks, snacks, and games like nude Twister to keep us entertained."

"It's not a camping trip."

Stretch appeared, sitting on the armrest between the two of them. *"Ask him if he's carrying."*

"Of course, he is," Ryley said.

"I am what? Who's here now?"

"My spirit guide, who also happens to be a stripper and my best friend."

He raised a brow. "Your best friend is a ghostly stripper?"

"And she asked if you were carrying a weapon."

"*No, I didn't.*" Stretch grinned. "*You're in for a long cozy night. You should see if he's got condoms.*"

"I am not asking him that." Ryley gawked and turned back to watch the scenery out the side window.

"Asking me what?" Keller asked.

"It doesn't matter. We aren't getting frisky tonight."

Keller's cheeks tinted. "She wanted to know if I've got condoms?"

"Of course. She thinks you'll put on a great show."

"She watches people having sex?" Keller asked with widened eyes.

"Everyone needs a hobby. I think she scores each performance on a scale of one to ten."

"I don't even want to know," he said with a shake of his head.

It was probably best that he didn't. Having a ghost watch you getting busy wasn't fun for anyone at all, especially when the ghost in question kept yelling out tips, and the score.

"*I've already looked in his backpack. I guess it's true what they say; lawmen are prepared for pretty much anything.*" Stretch chuckled.

"I'm sure you know it's true from experience," Ryley said.

"It's like I'm only hearing one side of a telephone conversation."

"It's not important."

"Well, since you've got friends going with us, maybe they can save us the trouble and tell us who is haunting the place and what happened and we can go home early," Keller said.

"Even if she wanted to, she can't," Ryley answered.

"Why not? Can't they like go through walls and stuff and talk to other spirits?"

"There is some type of barrier about the place or the land. I'm not really sure yet."

"How do you know that? Did you get a feeling?"

"No, your grandmother and Tessa couldn't get past the gate. Something is seriously wrong with that place."

10

After carrying the supplies into the house, both she and Keller got a chance to look around even more. The place had power and running water, even if the water looked a little suspicious and the lights in certain places were already flickering.

Neither Keller nor she was convinced the ghosts were causing it or if it couldn't just be explained away as crappy electrical in need of repair.

The downstairs bathroom was furnished with toilet paper as if that was the one Amanda had been using. The house had a very different vibe during this visit.

It was quiet. Almost too quiet, like the ghosts around the corners were waiting to pounce.

Keller pulled the sheets off of the two couches near the fire. Dust floated in the air.

"We can sleep on these," he offered.

"You can sleep on those. I'm not," Ryley answered, heading back outside to grab her sleeping bag from his trunk. She carried it back in.

"You can take the cot. I'll use your sleeping bag and sleep on the floor."

She dropped her bag next to the cot and unzipped her backpack, taking out a flashlight and setting it next to her things.

"What's that for? We have light," Keller said as if confused.

"Yeah, well, we don't know how old the electricity is in this place. Ghosts use whatever energy is nearby. This way, we're prepared."

"There's nothing wrong with that."

She headed for the stairs, her gaze on the landing above, waiting to see if anyone or anything decided to pop out.

The light overhead flickered, proving her point. "Are we even sure it's safe to be in this house?"

He shrugged. "I haven't asked."

"And what about forensics? Did they search for evidence?" she asked.

"That's what I'm told. The sheriff was personally out here dealing with the case."

"Great. I'm sure they're best friends." Ryley glanced up the stairs. "Any idea what balcony Amanda was pushed off of?"

"Master suite," he said, following her up and stopping at the top of the landing and looking both ways.

"Which way is that?"

"Your guess is as good as mine."

"Perfect. I'll check down this hallway, and you check the other."

"We'll go together. Shadow, remember?"

She held her arms out to her side. "Frisk me now and get it out of your system. I'm not taking you to the bathroom with me later."

He stepped behind her and ran his hands down her arms, her sides, and her legs before stepping back. "You're clean."

"Perfect. Now maybe I can move around the house without you breathing down my neck."

"You don't think we should stick together? There's more protection in pairs."

"We want these ghosts to come out to play. I have a feeling they aren't going to do it with an audience."

"Suit yourself. I'm going to look for the balcony. I didn't see any out front, so the room in question must be facing the backyard. Holler if you get scared."

As if. She headed back down the stairs. "Let's start on the first floor and work our way up to the balcony."

"You go ahead."

She jogged down the stairs and walked into the kitchen. It was still too light outside for much to happen. She took her time surveying the kitchen area. Spacious. Updated.

She moved on down a hallway off the kitchen and came to a small room. A single bed sat in the corner. The walls were bare. Nothing ornate about the room. A wooden rocking chair sat in another corner of the room.

"Maid or chef," she said, stepping inside.

The closet was empty, without so much as a hanger. She walked into the adjoining bathroom. The wallpaper was yellowing. A film covered the mirror. The clawfoot tub was rusted and in need of replacing.

Creak. Creak. Creak.

The sound made Ryley still and strain to hear more.

Creak. Creak. Creak.

A chill skirted her arms. Was that the rocking chair in the bedroom? Finally. Someone was there to play.

She stepped back into the room. The rocking chair was still in motion. Only there wasn't a ghost sitting in it. Keller was rocking back and forth. "This thing is great. My mom would have loved this."

"She liked old things?"

"Antiques. She collected them," he answered.

"I found the balcony and some more creepy things upstairs in the room if you want to take a look."

Hunting ghosts was so much easier when she did it by herself. She bit back her annoyance. "Lead the way."

She followed him up to the second floor. He stopped at the first door and gestured for her to go inside.

French doors gave way to a balcony outside.

"Looks like the balcony goes the entire length of the back of the house," Keller said as if answering her unasked question.

The room had been a child's room. A pink four-poster princess bed sat perched against the wall as if this room was special for a little princess.

"Bateman's adoptive kid, maybe?" she asked.

"Are we sure the Batemans were the last owners? I don't recall reading in the file that they had kids."

"They were. The name was still on the mailbox."

"Observant."

"It helps keep me alive."

She followed Keller into the next room. It was decorated much like the first, only for a boy instead. Trophies lined the dresser for some type of horse-riding competition and rowing. Medals hung on the side of the mirror.

Keller went straight to the balcony door and opened it as Ryley peeked inside the closet. Creepy rows of school uniforms still hung on the hangers as if frozen in time.

"Come take a look at this," Keller called out.

A brief chill caressed her arms. Even if she couldn't see the spirit, she realized again she wasn't alone. Outside, Keller had walked down the length of the balcony and gestured to the last room. "Master suite is down here. Looks like they took fingerprints from the balcony and the door."

"Because ghosts leave fingerprints," she grumbled and glanced over the edge. "I'm surprised a freak fall like that didn't kill her."

"Maybe the bushes broke her fall."

Those weren't just bushes. Those were holly

bushes. Not only did they hurt; they also left scratches. Ryley's mother used to have some planted outside her room to stop her from sneaking out.

Ryley shook the railing. It was loose and wobbly. No way would she have been leaning over it to look at anything. "It's not very secure."

He jiggled it as if to test it for himself. "We need to stay away from that."

She tried to open the door to go into the master suite. It didn't budge. "The cops must have locked up when they left. Looks like we have to go back through the boy's room."

Swish, slam.

She heard it before she realized what was happening.

Her mouth parted even as Keller stared at her with dipped brows. "What the hell was that?"

"Nothing good, I can tell you that," she said, jogging down to the boy's room to find the door had closed. She turned the handle to find it locked. "We're locked out. Where's your gun? Shoot out the window."

"It's locked in the car!"

"Why the heck would you leave it there?"

"Momentary lapse of judgment, thinking there

wouldn't be any threats in an empty house. It's not like I can shoot the ghosts even if I could see them."

"Valid point. You're forgiven."

"You think someone is in there?" he asked.

Ryley cupped her hands to see through the dirty glass. "No one living."

"Perfect. One of these has to be unlocked." He went quickly up and down the balcony, checking the doors to see if any of the others would offer a way inside. "Nothing. Damn it."

Ryley tried the master suite door again, to no avail. "Do you think that's what Amanda was doing out here? You think a ghost lured her or locked her out and she fell trying to get down?"

"Your guess is as good as mine. Last I checked, she hasn't woken up yet. Did you bring your phone out here?"

She shook her head. "It's in my bag. What about you?"

He patted his chest as if checking his pockets. "Mine is downstairs in my jacket."

"Okay then," she said. "This could be worse. I could still be in that damn skirt and heels from this morning. Is there anything out here that can break one of the glass panes?"

He went up and down the balcony, looking while

she turned her gaze to their only other option. She glanced over the railing, looking down at the ground below and what might be up above. There was no way to tell if anything was even open or unlocked on the floor above.

One way or another, they were getting back inside.

"There's nothing out here." He yanked off his tie and began to unbutton his shirt.

"I'm all for wasting time, but maybe we should wait since the condoms are in your backpack." She shrugged. "What the hell. It might just relieve some stress. I'm game." She reached for the button on her jeans.

"What are you doing?" He balked in confusion.

"I don't know. You're getting undressed. I thought maybe we could tie our clothes together and you could lower me down."

His lips twisted in disbelief. "As fun as that sounds, first let me wrap my hand and arm to see if I can break the windowpane with my elbow. If that doesn't work, we'll have to revisit the naked climb."

She stopped her striptease, kind of glad she wasn't getting all the way naked. Nothing about her undergarments screamed "sex me all night long," but they did kind of work for a "hey, throw me off the balcony" scenario.

He wrapped his arm several times in his crisp white button-down shirt and then slammed his elbow against the glass door.

Nothing happened except his goofy grin was replaced with a look of pain.

She kicked the loose railing. It bounced off the holly bushes and landed on the porch with a clatter.

"What the hell are you doing?" he asked, putting his shirt back on but rolling up his sleeves.

"Looks like there's only one way back inside." She sat on her tush with her feet dangling over the edge. "If I lower myself, I'll be halfway down. I can jump the rest of the way."

"You'll fall and break your damn neck," he growled.

"We're out of options unless, of course, you want to wait to be rescued tomorrow, should Judge Henley bother to come looking for us."

She was already maneuvering her weight over the edge of the porch. Concrete dug into her hands and fingertips as she tried to get a good grip.

Her fingers were slipping with each passing second.

She kicked her feet, looking for anything at all to

get a footing, unsure if a vine or trellis was within reach.

Nothing besides the bushes below.

Fingers wrapped tightly around her wrist, and she glanced up to find Keller lying on his stomach with his tight grip on her wrist. "Nice and easy, and I'll help lower you as far as I can, but you're going to have to jump the rest of the way."

"Shouldn't be too bad," she lied as she glanced down. "Just help me dodge the killer bush below."

11

No amount of chilly breeze could stop the sweat that beaded on Ryley's brow as she dangled what felt like miles above the earth. She'd scaled much higher balconies at a younger age and fallen off a few. She'd been scared of heights ever since, but she wasn't really that high off the ground. This should have been an easy jump.

"I'm going to swing you out so that you land on the grass. Try your best to miss the bushes and the railing you knocked off, or I'll have to take you in for a tetanus shot."

"No worries. I won't feel a shot in my broken arm. Think I can sue the home owner's insurance?"

Keller's concentration never waned.

"Are you ready?" His voice was turning more

strained by the second, as if her weight was getting to be too much.

She glanced over her shoulder and down once more, trying to gauge where exactly she wanted to go. There was no good place. Not unless she could clear the bushes.

"I'm ready."

"I'll let go on the count of three." He began to swing her as if she were a gymnast who had full confidence in her partner and ability to stick the landing.

"One. Be sure to tuck and roll."

If she broke her leg, then what the hell would they do?

"Two."

Would she have to crawl around to the front door? And who was to say that it, too, wasn't locked. She wouldn't have keys to drive anywhere to get...

"Three."

A scream bubbled free from her lips as Keller's grip on her wrists fell away and she went flying over the bushes.

She forgot to tuck and roll, landing painfully on her arm and knocking the wind out of her body. Pain shot through her shoulder and arm as she lay motionless, trying to breathe.

"Ryley, talk to me," Keller yelled.

"I'm good." She took a deep breath. "I just need a minute."

"If you're good, then how come you're not moving?" Panic laced his voice.

Tears welled in her eyes. The adrenaline and shock of what had happened subsided and made way for the pain to take hold.

She rolled onto her back, grabbing her arm to still it from sudden movements. Clenching her eyes closed, she breathed through the pain, knowing that she'd fractured something.

She eased up to a sitting position and glanced up at him. "I'm going to need a doctor."

"Damn it, Ryley. I can't do anything from up here. Can you make it to the front door?"

She tried to stand, and pain shot up into her leg from her foot. She took a step, one and then two, trying to keep weight off of her foot. She collapsed before trying again.

"Don't go anywhere. I'll get there, eventually," she called out. She would have laughed at her joke if the pain hadn't stolen her humor.

It took longer than expected to get around the house, with the overgrown underbrush in the way. Rounding the house, she hobbled up onto the porch and twisted the knob, thankful that the ghost had forgotten to lock all the doors.

She went inside, grabbed her chirping phone, and slid it into her pocket before hopping up the stairs to the boy's room, resting every couple of steps.

Keller was pacing on the patio. She unlocked the door, and he shoved it open, barely letting her get out of the way.

"Where does it hurt?" he asked, pulling a leaf from her hair.

"I landed on my arm. I'm pretty sure it's probably fractured, and I think I hurt my foot."

The words had barely left her mouth when he scooped her up in his arms and carried her back down the stairs, easing her down, only long enough to grab his gun, badge, and the car keys.

He hoisted her up again and carried her to the SUV, not letting her feet touch the ground before settling her in the passenger seat.

He started the SUV. "I'll be right back."

She nodded and leaned her seat backward, staring up at the ghost in the window, which was staring back at her.

The trip to the hospital would have been comical if she wasn't in pain. He didn't seem to be worried about the speed limit signs, ignoring each one he passed.

When blue lights flashed in the newly forming darkness, he groaned and whipped out his badge before the officer even made it to the window.

"I need to get her to the nearest hospital, and we need a police escort."

"No, we don't," Ryley whispered.

The officer nodded and did exactly what Keller had asked.

She could just hear it now. The cop would need to call in the fact that he was running lights and sirens, and the rest of the precinct would know it had something to do with her.

A nurse was waiting with a wheelchair when they pulled up into the ER, as if the cop had called ahead of time to warn them that an emergency was on the way.

Ryley was whisked into a room. When Keller tried to follow, the EMTs told him he had to park somewhere else. She lost sight of him after that.

"You must be important, honey," the orderly said as he pushed the wheelchair down the hall.

"I'm no one."

He turned the corner into one of the rooms. "Now that's not true. You got a police escort and were brought in by the FBI. What kind of trouble did you get into that got you all banged up?"

"You wouldn't believe me if I told you."

She was saved from having to answer him when a doctor walked in, followed by a nurse, effectively kicking the orderly out.

She hated hospitals, and for a good reason. She'd already passed not one ghost but three. And the worst part was that Amanda's confused spirit was currently standing in the room.

"He got you too, didn't he?"

He? Who was he?

12

The door opened, and a doctor with salt and pepper hair walked in wearing a white coat with a stethoscope draped around his neck.

The swish of the door and the newcomers were so quick that it scared Amanda's spirit straight out of the room.

"I'm Dr. Rinehart, and I hear you, young lady, had a police escort."

"I'm Ryley, and you say that like it's unusual to have a police escort." Ryley grimaced in pain.

"We see all kinds here," he said, reaching for her arm as he asked the question, "What seems to be the problem?"

"I hurt my arm," she answered as he poked and prodded.

"And how did you do this?" he asked.

"I jumped from a second-story balcony."

"Is that like a social media viral thing now? You're the second that I've seen."

Was this guy Amanda's doctor?

"I'm betting it's the same balcony if you're referring to Amanda Greenly."

He frowned but kept looking at her arm. "Friend of yours?"

"Nope, but the same balcony," Ryley answered.

He looked up as if startled by her words. "Seems you fared much better than she did."

"I tucked and rolled," Ryley lied.

"Hmm." He lowered his head again and moved to her foot, easing off her shoe. "Are you sure you jumped and the same person didn't push you? This is a safe place; you can tell us what really happened."

As if.

"It's a long story. The FBI agent that brought me in should be in here any minute. He witnessed the whole thing and can tell you all about it."

The door opened, and Keller stepped inside, flashing his badge at the doctor. "Is she going to live?"

"Not sure of the damage yet. We're going to need to get her x-rayed to be sure. It's going to be a while, if you've got somewhere else to be. We can call you when we're done."

"Nope, I'm good." He planted himself in a chair across the room as if ready to lay down roots.

"Sir, the nurse is going to need to help Ryley change into a hospital gown."

"Right." He popped up and met Ryley's gaze. "I'll be right outside the door and come back in when you're done."

"Shadow." Ryley chuckled.

"Shadow," he agreed.

"Nurse Stein is going to help you change, and then we'll get you into x-ray for your arm and your foot."

"Thank you, Doctor," she called out to him as he was ushering Keller out the door.

The nurse made haste in getting Ryley changed without her having to move much to get into the hospital gown. She pulled up the wheelchair and helped her hobble over to it.

An hour later, she'd been x-rayed, poked and prodded, and filled out a mountain of paperwork. Luckily, the cop that had brought her in obviously hadn't told all the others about who needed the escort, or others would have shown up out of morbid curiosity just to give her a hard time.

Her clavicle had taken the brunt of the damage. The hairline fracture would heal over time once her arm and shoulder were stabilized. Her sprained foot was in need of ice, elevation, and minor pain meds. It would start to feel tender and get better in a few days if she kept her weight off of it. Not that her latest assignment was going to let her sit down long enough to let the healing powers take effect.

How was she supposed to expel ghosts from a seated position? Not to mention tending the bar with a sore foot and a bad arm. This was a first.

Thoughts of texting Oscar made her stomach tighten. If he or her brother, Tucker, ever found out exactly why or how this had happened, they might try to take matters into their own hands, and going up against Henley wasn't good for any of them.

After changing back into her clothes with her foot wrapped and a sling on her arm, she was re-dressed and in the wheelchair being pushed toward the ER's waiting room.

Keller had tried to take the chair from Nurse Stein, but the look she gave him had him holding up his hands in surrender.

She thought they were free and clear until the ER doors opened. Oscar and her brother were waiting nervously across the room.

They watched as she was wheeled out the exit, and Nurse Stein helped her out of the seat and onto a bench while they all stood around staring dumbfounded at her.

"Well, one of you men should probably go get a vehicle," Nurse Stein snapped.

"Right," Keller said. "That would be me."

"Oh, I think you've done enough. She'll be leaving with me," Oscar announced.

"Technically, I'm the only blood relative," Tucker said.

Nurse Stein met her gaze. "Ryley, would you like me to call you a cab?"

"That won't be necessary." Ryley smiled up at the woman. The pain medication from earlier had clearly kicked in. "I've got this under control."

"Okay, then." The nurse pulled the wheelchair back toward the sliding doors, giving each of the guys a dirty look as she went.

"Henley said she has to stay with me," Keller said in defense.

"Screw the judge. She was hurt," Tucker fired back.

"On your watch, Mr. FBI Man," Oscar added.

"You know, if we're going to fight about this, can

we do it at the diner? I could really use some apple pie."

"Apparently, aggravating people isn't the only thing that makes you hungry," Keller mumbled beneath his breath.

"Nope, almost dying because of a ghost ranks up there as a close second."

"Second?" Oscar chuffed. "The last time a ghost tried to kill you, you ate pie for a week straight."

"This has happened more than once?" Keller asked.

"Well, if you must know, I bring out the best in people, dead and alive." She turned her gaze to Oscar. "And as for eating pie for a week, I was milking it for what it's worth, but I'm in need… now." She frowned. "FBI can drive me home, since I need a shower. Oscar can follow, and Tucker can pick up pizza and the apple pie. He is the blood relative."

"Ryley. You aren't going back." Tucker crossed his arms over his chest.

"Sure, I am, and we're going to need sustenance while we strategize how to burn that house to the ground."

"I'm going to pretend I didn't hear that," Keller said, walking off toward his illegally parked SUV.

"He likes to pretend to be clueless," she told the others. "But I'm convinced it's just an act."

Tucker frowned. "Ryley, if I'd known…"

"Nothing would have changed," she told him. "I won't let this haunted house ruin your career or your cases." She turned to Oscar. "And I won't let this stupid judge overturn Wilson's will and give the estate to that nasty cousin."

Oscar gasped. "He wouldn't."

"Oh, he would, all right."

"No wonder you're helping them. You did all this for us."

Things were probably going to get worse. Way worse, now that Amanda had died.

How was she going to tell them when Ryley was no closer to giving Henley any answers?

Knowing her luck, the grieving judge would still be true to his word and destroy them all.

13

The farm was quiet. The one place Ryley could let down her guard, especially since she'd salted every possible entrance and exit point. No one was going to bother her sleep for at least one night.

"Listen, I'm sorry about earlier. I should have been the one to jump."

"It's not like I gave you a choice," Ryley said.

"True," Keller agreed. "I guess that really does make this your fault."

She opened the door, sliding out of the SUV just as Oscar pulled up and parked.

"Wait for a second and let me help you." Keller hurried out and rounded the car.

He bent down to pick her up, and she swatted his hands away.

"I don't need curb service. I just need a crutch, and you'll do." She grimaced, holding on to his arm, taking her time to maneuver up the stairs and through the front door. Oscar had the door open, blocking Ringwald and calming him as she slowly approached.

Ryley scratched the dog's head in passing as she stepped inside and headed for the stairs, only for Oscar to turn her away.

"You'll take a shower down here. I'll grab your things and a change of clothes."

"You afraid I won't come back downstairs?"

"No, I'm afraid you will." He grinned. "Without help."

"And if you fall in the shower, we won't be able to hear you," Keller added.

Oscar jogged up the stairs.

"Your invitation into my shower only extends if you're prepared to wash my back and shave my legs." No way was he coming in. This guy wasn't interested in her. It was why she was having so much fun at his expense. She maneuvered him down the hall to one of the guest bedroom's adjoining bathrooms.

"Nice place," he said.

"Glad you like it. You'll be sleeping here tonight."

"I couldn't do that. I have a hotel room."

"Shadow." She eased down on the bed, waiting for Oscar to return with her things.

Keller had been using that as an excuse the entire day. Now it was her turn. "If you need to run and get your things after dinner, feel free. It's not like I can go run a scam or anything while you're gone. I probably won't be running for a few days."

"I'll wait until after we eat and get a plan together." He headed for the door and turned at the last minute. "Preferably, one that doesn't include burning down the judge's property."

The suggestion was sounding better by the minute.

Oscar sidestepped Keller. "I put a pot of coffee on in the kitchen."

"I guess that's my cue." Keller chuckled, patting his pocket with a frown.

"We have a phone you can use. Oscar can show you."

Oscar stepped out of the bathroom after placing her toiletries and clothes inside. He frowned as he stared down at her. "You want me to stay and help?"

"No. I can manage."

His frown deepened as his gaze dropped to her arm. "This should have never happened."

"But it did, and I survived, so don't give him a

hard time. I was already hanging off the ledge before he could stop me. I guess I'm just a poor judge of distance." She hobbled to stand and took her time using the nearby furniture to help limp toward the bathroom.

"You think?" Oscar said as he shut the bathroom door. "He should have been keeping a closer eye on you."

"Because we really want that?" she called out.

"You make a valid point."

"I have my moments." She grinned.

Showering was more difficult than she'd expected. Only having one hand to unwrap her foot had been the start of her trouble.

It had taken her twice as long as her normal showers. She'd barely dressed when a knock sounded on the bathroom door.

"Ryley, you okay? You need help?" Oscar asked.

"Maybe with wrapping my foot," she said.

"Are you decent?"

"Yeah, I'm coming out." She opened the door, using every wall and counter in her reach to help keep her upright.

"You have a thing." Oscar tried to hold back his smile and pointed to her hair.

"My brush got stuck, and I twisted wrong or

moved my shoulder, and I started hurting again, so I just left it."

"May I?"

"I don't know. I was thinking I might make this trendy."

"That's never going to happen," he said, helping her to sit on the bed.

He untangled the brush from her hair, making her wince more than when she moved her arm the wrong way. Tears formed in her eyes even as she tried to hide the pain. A mixture of aggravation, helplessness, and just plain being pissed off about Henley had set her on an emotional ledge that she was close to falling over.

How had she let her life get this convoluted?

"You're stronger than that," Oscar said as if reading her mind. "And you have a secret weapon."

She wiped the free-falling tear. "Yeah, and what's that?"

"An arsenal full of ghosts and resources that are willing to help at a moment's notice. You are Wilson Foundation. I don't think you grasp exactly what that means yet."

"I know I don't say it enough, but I appreciate you."

"I know."

Oscar grinned and dropped to his knees and began wrapping her foot like he'd done it a million times before.

"You're a pro at that."

"I have experience. The pizza and apple pie arrived five minutes ago."

"Did he bring my favorite?" she asked, using him to pull herself off the bed.

"Yes. The house smells like pineapples and ham."

14

Oscar had found a crutch from goodness knows where. Her guess was somewhere out in the barn where he still kept some of Old Man Wilson's boxed-up property. Boxes that she'd one day have to deal with. Out of sight, out of mind was her motto.

She hobbled, using the crutch and her good foot to balance her way down the hallway. When she turned toward the kitchen, she stopped in her tracks, narrowing her eyes as she glanced over her shoulder toward the front door.

"What's wrong? Did you forget something?"

"Yeah, I forgot to warn them about my salt lines."

"I can add more," he offered.

"No, unless you plan to sage first. They're already back in the house."

"Who is?"

"Everyone," Ryley said, hobbling toward the kitchen where Ada Mae was pacing. Stretch was hovering as if she were sitting on the counter, and Tessa was sitting on the floor with her back to the wall like a bored teen.

"Oh, thank goodness. She saved my grandson," Ada Mae said, clutching her necklace.

"At least she saved someone," Tessa mumbled.

"I can see why she did," Stretch said seductively.

Ryley ignored them all, hobbling further into the kitchen.

It was pitch-black outside and almost two in the morning. She was exhausted. She hadn't planned for a ghost hunting expedition last time she slept, or she would have accounted for it with an extra nap.

Keller was eating a piece of pepperoni pizza. Tucker was feeding a part of his crust to Ringwald. Neither man said a word to the other.

"What, no fighting about who's going to make me a plate?"

Keller shoved up from his chair when Oscar chuckled. "Sit down."

He sat without much prompting. His tired eyes raked over Ryley, and he watched every move she made until she took a seat across from him.

Oscar put a drink and a plate in front of her. She grabbed two slices and devoured an entire piece before she even spoke.

"Okay, first of all, everyone needs to respect my salt lines. I keep them for a reason."

Keller frowned. Tucker's eyes widened.

"Sorry, Ryley. That was probably me. I wiped my feet," Tucker admitted.

"It's okay. I'll get them all out again when I have full use of my faculties."

"Have you figured out who is haunting Henley's house and hurt Amanda and how to get rid of them?" Tucker asked, taking a bite of his pizza.

"I'm sure it's the same one that locked us out," Keller said.

She didn't know how to tell them the secret she was carrying, surprised that Henley hadn't called Keller yet.

"Here's the thing." She wiped her mouth and took a sip of her drink. "It's only going to be worse from here on out, Tuck. You need to start pulling records to show that I wasn't involved with anyone's case but Bane's, Crews' mother, and Jennings. My guess is the judge is going to hit swift and hard."

"I agree. I'm glad you're backing out. You can

tell him tomorrow that you got hurt, too, and you don't want to do it. We'll survive the fallout," Tucker said.

Poor guy had no idea.

"Tuck, I'm not going to back off. I'm going to rid that house of ghosts."

"But you just said..." Tuck questioned.

"I saw another spirit today while in the hospital."

"Who?" Keller asked.

Oscar sighed as if he'd figured out the only spirit who mattered most in this situation.

"Amanda. She appeared in my room at the ER."

"No, she's not dead. She can't be," Tucker said. "She survived the fall, just like you did."

"You're wrong," Keller said, shoving out of his chair. He pulled out his phone and dialed it as he left the room. Seconds later, they heard the front door slam.

"What's his problem?" Oscar asked.

Ryley shrugged. "Maybe he's pissed he has to go back to real work."

"That's not it," Tucker said, standing up and walking to the fridge. He grabbed a beer and retook his seat. "Do you remember the reason why Amanda broke up with me?"

"Yeah, she was seeing the judge," Ryley offered.

Tucker took a swig of his beer. "The judge came later. She broke up with me because of Keller."

"Wait, what? Are you saying that he's the guy that stole her away?" Ryley growled.

"Makes perfect sense now. When both of you are near each other, it's ice cold," Oscar said.

"He didn't tell me that." Ryley folded her arms over her chest. "If I thought for a minute, I was doing it for him, now knowing who the *him* is, then I wouldn't have agreed." Ryley's jaw flexed as her blood pressure started to rise to knew heights.

"It wasn't him who asked," Tucker said, handing her his beer.

She took a good, long swig and handed it back.

"Well, there goes the farm. Now you can't operate any heavy machinery with painkillers *and* alcohol in your system," Oscar said.

"Damn. Guess after I eat, I'm going to have to go to bed." Ryley smirked.

"Is she really dead?" Tucker asked.

Ryley nodded. "She asked if the ghost got the better of me too, and then she vanished when others came into the room."

"Damn," Tuck said, resting his hands on the counter and staring out into the darkness. "I never wanted that to happen to her."

The door opened and slammed again. Keller yelled through the house as he walked back into the kitchen. "Why in the hell would you do that?"

"Oh, dear. He never sounds that mad. Someone must have really upset him," Ada Mae said.

"Good, now maybe we can get on to saving my sister's life before she's the next victim," Tessa said.

"You can always kiss and make up. I've done it several times. A man forgets his anger when you show him your tender side," Stretch added.

"Oh, you three shut it. There is nothing tender about me, and no way in hell am I going to be yelled at in my own damn house," Ryley growled at them.

Turning her anger toward Keller, she continued. "You better watch your tone, Special Agent Keller. I'm not the one keeping secrets here. How could you steal Amanda from my brother?"

"Is that what this is about? Some sick, twisted revenge. Let's just tell him Amanda is dead when she isn't."

Ryley paused. "What do you mean, she isn't? I saw her spirit. She even talked to me."

"Yeah, well. You're wrong. Amanda Greenly isn't dead. She's in a medically induced coma. I just verified it with Henley and the hospital."

Ryley's mouth parted. How was that possible?

"Maybe she died for only a second and they resuscitated her. Hell, I don't know. What I do know is I saw her in spirit form in the ER. I don't know what else to tell you." Ryley dismissively shook her hands. That so wasn't the point. "Regardless, you didn't tell me about your relationship with Amanda."

"It was irrelevant."

"Don't let him lie to you, dear. She was the reason he was in town before her accident," Ada Mae announced.

"Grandmother, just stop it. You're making things worse," Keller growled and turned in her direction.

The entire room turned silent. Ryley gasped, and her hand flew over her mouth.

"Grandmother?" Oscar asked.

Ryley pointed to the corner where Ada Mae was standing. "Well, well, well." She dropped her hand. "What other secrets are you hiding, Keller? You were here to see Amanda and now come to find out that you can also see ghosts. Why the hell didn't you tell me that? That's something relevant to share."

"Ryley." Keller frowned.

"Save it. I don't care what your excuse is. I don't care why you were here to see Amanda. I don't even care that you kept it a secret. What I do care about is getting this over with, finding the ghost that locked us out on the balcony, and getting Henley off my back and out of my life." She grabbed the crutch and crossed the room to stand in front of him. "This ends tomorrow."

She rounded him and headed out of the kitchen toward the stairs. "And when you leave, you need to take your grandmother with you."

"Ryley, wait!" Oscar called out. "Why don't we all just calm down and have some pie."

"You all can eat the damn pie. I'm going to bed and in my own room without my damn shadow." Ryley hobbled to the stairs and took her time, letting the anger fuel her body as she maneuvered the steps.

In her room, she put the crutch against the dresser and climbed up onto her bed, not even bothering to pull the covers back. Grabbing a blanket at the bottom of the bed, she haphazardly covered herself and turned to lie on her good arm while cradling the bad.

She'd get rid of the ghost one way or another tomorrow, if she had to pay someone to burn that damn house to the ground and salt every inch of the ground. With that thought, she closed her eyes and let the darkness suck her thoughts away.

15

Ryley woke when she heard her door creak open and the smell of coffee entered the room.

"You didn't knock," she said, rolling onto her side.

"I guess I'm in tune with your sleep schedule." Oscar put the coffee mug on the table next to her and helped her sit up.

He handed her a painkiller and a glass of water, waiting for her to take it, and then handed her the coffee.

"Your friendship was the best thing to come out of Wilson's estate."

"You sure it wasn't the money?" Oscar teased, going into the closet. He returned with a button-up shirt that would be easy for her to maneuver in and out of and a pair of stretchy pull-up yoga pants that didn't require buttons or much of a struggle.

"I'm sure. I'm just sorry that you're now part of my train wreck."

"I'm happy right where I am," Oscar said, going to the door. "Finish your coffee and leave your cup up here. I'll get it later. When you get dressed, meet me in the library so we can figure out who these ghosts are."

"What about Keller?"

"He's downstairs, asleep in one of the spare rooms. He and your brother had a few too many beers and hashed things out."

Ryley's eyes widened. "Did it come to blows?"

Oscar grinned. "Maybe."

"You let me miss it?" She chuckled.

"Well, you were adamant about going to bed." He grinned. "I didn't let them touch your pie. I'll heat you up a slice, and you can have it for breakfast."

"Thanks, mom." Ryley teased as Oscar shut the door.

Resting her head against the headboard, she sipped the coffee, enjoying the peacefulness she'd been lacking for the last twenty-four hours.

Thirty minutes later, she'd made her way into the

library, and good to his word, Oscar had a piece of hot pie and another cup of coffee waiting on her.

"Have a seat." He gestured to the couch he'd brought in.

"When did you have time to move furniture?"

"When you went to bed, I continued to research the Batemans. I thought we'd powwow in here."

"Great."

She sat on the couch, and an ottoman appeared in front of her with a pillow on top of it. Oscar lifted her foot onto the pillow and grabbed a towel and ice pack, gently laying it atop.

She took a second and said a silent prayer for all the goodness and everything she was grateful for in her life. If ghosts killed her today, it was going to be with a semi-clear conscience and partially positive karma.

"You spoil me," she said, offering him a bite of her pie.

He declined. "I already had a piece last night while I was researching. I deserved it."

"You deserve more than that for dealing with me." Ryley's phone vibrated in her pocket. "Hang on."

She jostled one-handed and finally put her pie down and dug her phone out of her pocket.

Now is a good time. I can meet you at Tessa's sister's home. I'd like to be there when you talk to her.

Henry had actually followed through on his promise.

Just send me the address and time, and I'll meet you there, she texted back.

Another text with the address and time, which was less than thirty minutes from then, appeared on her phone.

"You're going to have to hold your thoughts on how to evict the ghosts. I have something important to do."

"More important than this?" Oscar asked.

"I saved my own life yesterday. Today I'm saving someone else."

"Where are you going?" he asked, following her as she hobbled down the hall.

"To meet Henry at Tessa's sister's house," she said.

"How are you going to do that? You can't drive. Wait here and let me grab my keys," Oscar offered.

"I'll take her," Keller said, appearing freshly rested from the spare room. "I'm supposed to be shadowing her, anyway."

"You don't even know where she's going."

"She's going to deal with Tessa's family to get the

ghost to cross into the light. She's been following us the entire time."

"That's right. I forgot you could see them too," Oscar said.

"In my line of work, it's not openly discussed around outsiders."

He had a point. She wouldn't have told anyone either, if circumstances had been different.

"Let me grab her spare backpack in case she needs it."

"Salt and sage?" he asked.

"Yeah."

"Don't bother. I have some hidden in the trunk and another delivery on the way." He glanced at his watch. "It should be here by lunch."

"What delivery?" she asked.

"Not what. Who." He smiled. "We'll talk about it on the way."

"Keller, why do you carry salt and sage in your trunk? I mean I know why Ryley does, but why would you, when you're bent on hiding your ability?"

"I never leave home without it when staying in hotel rooms," Keller said, holding the door open for her. "You know this would be easier if I carried you."

"All of it would have been easier if I'd known you

could see Tessa and the others the whole time," she said, hobbling out the door.

"She's not here now. They all vanished when you yelled at us. How do you know she's going to show up?"

"They always do." Well, most of the time, but she didn't need to tell him that. They might have the same gift of seeing dead people, but could the FBI agent shove the spirits into the light? Or was that an ability only she'd obtained?

She wasn't about to ask. The quicker they did all this, the faster she could return to her own version of normal.

16

There was a tense, awkward quietness in the SUV as Keller drove toward town.

"I'm sorry I didn't tell you about Amanda. If I had, you wouldn't have worked the case on purpose, and then your brother's career and life really would have been screwed. I couldn't let that happen to him, not twice."

"Whatever helps you sleep at night," Ryley said, turning her gaze toward the window.

"I was twenty-one when I met Amanda and we started dating. I didn't know she was seeing your brother until after she broke up with him. At that age, we don't always see the bigger picture." He glanced her way. "Or make the best choices. Wouldn't you agree?"

"Don't pretend you grew a conscience and you want to find the ghost to save my brother more grief. This has nothing to do with why you're here and want this solved. It's more about you and Amanda. You still love her, don't you?"

"We separated years ago. We just never filed the paperwork. This is a technicality, and as for Amanda, I'll always love her; she was my wife."

"Wife? I thought you just dated." Ryley gawked.

"We were young." That was his only answer.

"I really did see her in the ER." Ryley turned to look at him. "You know what that potentially means, right?"

He nodded. "She had a complication. She flat-lined for three minutes until they brought her back. I was notified this morning when I updated Henley about what happened at his house."

"You told him I got hurt?"

"Yes. I even told him it's not a wise idea to let anyone else on the property."

"Bet he didn't like that."

"He disagreed and said if you and I couldn't get the job done, he'd go above our heads."

"Who exactly does he think is above my head? Does he think God won't let me in the pearly gates when I die? He's the only person that's higher than me, and sometimes I can still act like a disgruntled teen, ignoring parents' warnings and wishes."

"I can see that about you, but I think he was talking about my boss and, for you, probably destroying your brother. Now that I know he threatened you, honestly, I don't know what Amanda sees in him."

"Are you worried you'll get in trouble with your boss?"

Keller glanced her way. His eyes sparkled like he had more secrets. "No. My boss knows exactly how to handle men like Henley. That's why I called him first. He's sending in the cavalry."

It must have been nice to have backup in situations like this. She'd never met another psychic that could see the dead as easily as he could. Nor any that she'd ever had a conversation with.

"I'm sorry about Amanda. I don't hate her," Ryley said.

Keller chuckled. "She never hated you either, even when you convinced her you could see ghosts."

Heat flushed Ryley's cheeks. "I don't know what you're talking about. I don't think she was ever convinced."

"Sure, she was. She was scared out of her wits for months after you sent one of your cronies to get revenge for your brother. It's how she knew you were the real deal." He glanced at her. "It paved the way for me to share my secret with her."

"So glad I could help your relationship." Ryley rolled her eyes.

Keller chuckled but didn't reply.

"You know, near-death experiences can change a person. You realize that, right?"

"Yep. It's too early to tell what the outcome is going to look like for her, but if she needs me, I'll help her through it."

"I hope the date that's waiting for you understands the connection. You might want to come clean about it upfront." Ryley's phone called out the arrival at Ivy Murphy's house, and Keller parked at the curb.

It was a modest bungalow with a white picket fence. The grass and shrubs were in need of a trim but not to the point of being overgrown. A small, compact crossover SUV, which seemed several years old, sat in the driveway. Behind the SUV was a large white truck with a cross sticker on the windshield.

"Henry is already here." Ryley opened the door and slid out, keeping her weight on her good foot, until Keller grabbed the crutch and helped her through the fence and up to the door.

He knocked, and the door swung open. Henry stood on the threshold. He frowned as he met Keller's gaze and then turned to Ryley.

"I thought you were coming alone."

Ryley lifted the sling. "It wasn't possible."

"What happened to you? You look a little worse for the wear since the last time I saw you. Does this have anything to do with why you were escorted away from the funeral?"

"Henry, who is it? Is it your friend?" a woman asked from inside.

"Yes, Ivy. It's the woman I was telling you about." Henry held the door open.

Keller helped her up the step and into the cramped living room. "Ivy, this is Ryley St. James."

Ryley tilted her head toward Keller. "And this is my friend, FBI Special Agent Roger Keller."

"FBI?" Ivy grabbed the clothes basket off the couch and moved it out of the way. A baby was sitting in a crib holding a toy. "You didn't tell me the FBI was coming."

"I didn't know," Henry said.

"Come in. Let's have a seat." Ivy gestured to the living room couch.

Tessa was floating on her knees in front of the baby, making faces at the kid. "*I'm glad you're finally here. After all that fighting last night, I came here. I missed this little guy, and it looks like Justin missed me, too."*

"Tes, Tes, Tes, Tes," the baby kept repeating.

Ivy sighed. A sadness dulled her eyes. "Sorry, Tessa taught him that when she was trying to get him to say her name."

Ryley and Keller exchanged a look with each other as they took seats on one of the couches. Ivy sat in one of the chairs, and Henry pulled a chair from the small kitchen table.

"You'll have to excuse the mess. As you can imagine, I haven't had much time to clean," Ivy said.

"Not a problem. Sorry to drop in like this, but I'm afraid it couldn't be avoided." Ryley sighed and took a deep breath. "Do you know who I am?"

She shook her head. "Henry said that you attend funerals, and the newspapers said you're the new head of Wilson Foundation."

"You've heard of the foundation?"

"Of course. Everyone in town knows of the Wilson Foundation. Years ago, the foundation had a program for struggling single parents with grants and such for housing. I wouldn't have this house if it wasn't for them," Ivy said as pink tinted her cheeks.

"Forgive me, but your parents didn't help you?"

"No, I was unwed and pregnant, and let's just say that those two things together didn't measure up to their values."

"But it's different now?"

"Yeah, thanks to Tessa. When she left home and started college, she came to live with me, and six months ago, my parents came over to try to talk her into returning. That's when they got their first look at their grandbaby." Ivy glanced at Justin. "How could anyone ever say that child isn't a blessing straight from God himself? So, I have Tessa's defiance to thank for sort of mending the rift."

"Wow, if that had been my parents, I'm not so sure that I'd let them back in my life that quickly," Ryley said, thinking of her own father. No way in hell would she ever let him near her offspring, if she ever had any.

"It wasn't easy, and I don't know if it was the right decision, but I'm reserving judgment. I can tell you that I'll never let my parents hurt my child. He comes first. He'll always come first."

"You sound like my mom," Ryley said with a frown. It had been a month since she'd visited the gravesite in hopes of finally getting to see her mother. Not once had she shown herself to Ryley in all the years she'd been gone.

Ivy glanced at her watch. "I'm sure you didn't come here to talk about my parents."

"Actually, I came to talk about Tessa. She was worried about you."

The room turned silent, as if a pin drop would have been too loud. Ivy glanced up at Henry and then back at Ryley. "I don't understand. Tessa has never mentioned you. Did you meet her before she died?"

Tessa hovered near her sister but thankfully kept quiet, letting Ryley figure out how to tell her the truth. After several seconds of deliberation, she finally just blurted it out. "Not in life, but I met her at the funeral."

Ivy was out of her chair in an instant and picking up her son as if going into momma-bear protection mode.

"Is this some type of sick joke?"

Funny, some adults had the same reaction. Not all, but some. The most extreme believed Ryley would ruin their souls or give them some type of horrible affliction just for knowing that she could see ghosts and that death wasn't the end.

Didn't everyone realize that they had the same ability if they just tried? Talking to ghosts wasn't talking to the Devil. There was no sick, twisted game with these ghosts trying to steal her soul. These people needed help, and damn it, Ryley's ego would always take a back seat. Did that make her a bad person?

"No joke. Just trying to save your sister's soul and get her to move on."

17

"It's no joke. I can see dead people, and your sister is worried about you."

"Listen, I don't know what you're selling, but I'm not interested, and I have to get Justin to my mom's house."

"Your mother?" Henry asked.

"Tessa used to take turns babysitting him while I worked. She was working, too, and doing night classes. I haven't found someone else yet."

"It's understandable."

"She doesn't believe you. Make her believe," Tessa said, floating near them.

"I'm not here to cause you any trouble. Your sister is worried about you. I just needed to tell you so that her soul can be at peace."

"I miss her." Ivy swallowed and lifted her chin. "But I know she's in a better place. I know I'll see her again."

Tell her that I was murdered. Tell her the accident wasn't my fault. Tell her to stop asking questions and poking the wrong people or she's going to get hurt, too.

"She claims her accident wasn't an accident and that she was murdered. She also is saying that you need to stop asking questions and poking the wrong people or you'll get hurt, too."

"Ivy, is that true? I thought we'd agree that you'd let the police handle it."

Ryley's mouth parted. Ivy Murphy was already on to the fact that her sister's death wasn't an accident.

"They aren't doing anything. They aren't even working the case." Ivy's nostril flared. "They said it was an accident. They have no evidence to suggest it wasn't."

"How do you know that your sister's death wasn't an accident?" Keller asked, finally joining the conversation.

"Of course I do. Her car was just in the shop and repaired. She was kind of anal about Abigale."

"Who's Abigale?" Ryley asked.

"Her car. She named her car." Ivy sighed. "It was

her baby. That's how I knew something was wrong. No way was she speeding around Devil's Curve. She wasn't a speeder. She was like driving with my grandmother, always under the limit and afraid to get a ticket. She was the daughter that my parents always wanted. No way was the accident her fault. I'll never believe it."

That wasn't how Ryley heard it at the funeral. "Devil's Curve, that's where this happened?"

"I was speeding. I was being chased by the man in a black truck. He ran me off the road. I wasn't fast enough."

"Do you have any idea of who might have been following her? Maybe even ran her off the road? Anyone you can think of that would want to harm your sister?"

"No. No one. She would have told me if she was in trouble. She would have come to me. We're sisters. We've been taking care of each other all of our lives. There was foul play, I'm sure of it, but it wasn't Tessa's fault. I'll never believe that."

"If you can't think of anyone that would hurt your sister, why do you think there was foul play?"

"My sister doesn't speed."

She didn't elaborate any further.

"Obviously she did to get away from someone. Is her speeding the only reason you think foul play, or is there something more that you aren't telling us?"

"It was foul play. She wouldn't have been speeding. Haven't you been listening to me? She wouldn't have done that on purpose. There was something else wrong. That's why I called the mechanic."

"The mechanic?" Keller asked, sliding his hands into his pockets.

"Tessa had her car in the shop at Larry Stillman's garage. She'd just gotten it out that morning. He had to have missed something or maybe he sabotaged her brakes. I don't know. I just know it wasn't Tessa's fault. There is more going on."

"Oh, Ivy, you have to stop. I was speeding. I'm so sorry I died. I'm so sorry that I can't physically be here for you anymore. I'm so sorry."

"Your sister is really here. She's sorry that she died and can't be here for you."

A tear slipped down Ivy's face. "Please just leave. I thought since you were here with the FBI that you were here about her murder. Since you're not, please just go and leave me alone."

"You can't do that. She's going to keep looking for the answers and get killed, too," Tessa argued.

"Thank you for your time, Ms. Murphy. We'll see ourselves out."

"You can't go. Tell her to stop digging, or I swear to God, I'll never stop haunting you," Tessa growled.

Ryley was used to threats from the afterlife. She never paid that much attention to them. One way or another, she'd find a way to cross Tessa over.

"Tes, Tes, Tes." The baby held out his hands to where Tessa was hovering. It was him that made Ryley pause before she left at Ivy's request.

"Ivy, I believe she was run off the road. I'll look into it. I have friends on the police force. I have connections. I have the entire Wilson Foundation behind me. Let me do this for you and for her. Please stop searching for the answers. If not for me, or your sister, then for Justin. He really needs his mom, and I'm sure you don't want your parents raising him."

A look of horror crossed Ivy's face, as if the realization that was a possibility had struck her right smack between the eyes.

"She was my sister. How can I just let her go without knowing the truth? She deserves justice." A tear slid down Ivy's cheek.

"I'll find out the truth, one way or another. You have my word."

Ivy pressed a kiss onto Justin's forehead. The move looked like it soothed her just as much as the kid.

"We'll see ourselves out." Ryley hobbled out the door without looking back.

Keller remained quiet until they were both settled back in the SUV.

"Why did you promise her something you might not succeed in doing?"

"I don't plan to fail, even if I have to exhume Tessa and move her into the light myself."

"Wait, what did you mean, move her into the light?" he asked with pitched brows.

Damn. She hadn't meant to let that secret slip. She'd blurted out the first thing that popped into her mind. "I'll just have to convince Tessa that she doesn't have to worry. She can move on. What matters is that I'll get to the bottom of what happened, and if the cops won't take care of it..." She let the words hang, unwilling to incriminate herself.

"I'll pretend I didn't hear that."

Pretend away.

He started the SUV. "I guess if we're going to Larry Stillman's garage, you need to look it up on your phone and get directions. I'm sure I can shake some apples off the tree if you'd rather not go inside."

"I may be injured, but I'm never unarmed." She

pulled a pistol out of her sling to show him and then put it back.

"You have a permit for that?" he asked.

"Of course," she said matter-of-factly, trying to remember if she'd remembered to put it in her pocket. Maybe she shouldn't have shown Keller. "I'll be fine, and I'm ambidextrous. I can shoot with both hands."

His brows dipped. "Really?"

"You never know when that skill might come in handy. My boogeyman wouldn't be opposed to breaking my trigger finger."

Both her father and his criminal boss she'd put away with her testimony would break every finger on her hands if given the opportunity.

"When this is over, you and I will have a long talk about your boogeyman."

Not hardly. No way was she explaining to Keller about the evil in her own past, in her own family. Not happening.

Fifteen minutes later, Keller parked in front of Stillman's garage. A couple of mechanics were already underneath cars and working. The garage was attached to a convenience store on one side and a pizza restaurant on the other.

Men and women were parked in front of the

pumps, filling up their cars with gas, while others were carrying coffee as if starting their morning commutes.

Keller rounded the SUV and opened her door. She hobbled out and used the crutch for support as they entered the office area of the garage.

The smell of oil sat heavy in the air coming from the garage. A table fan was on and blowing on the receptionist, a woman with curly hair. Lipstick stained her coffee cup, and a pile of paperwork sat in the inbox.

The woman looked up from her conversation on the phone and smiled at Keller, dismissing Ryley altogether.

"I've got to call you back." She hung up, slowly rising. She batted her eyes. "Can I help you?"

Ryley smiled, waiting to see if Keller would flirt back to get the answers they needed.

He did the opposite.

Keller pulled out his badge and flashed it at the woman. "FBI Special Agent Roger Keller. Who can I talk to about vehicle repair records?"

"Sorry, hon, Larry won't let me give any of those out without a warrant. Client confidentiality and all that."

Laughter slipped free, and Ryley was quick to

recover. Client confidentiality about car repairs? Seriously?

Keller's lack of humor said enough.

"Sorry, I'll let you deal with that."

"Irene," he said, glancing at the nameplate in front of the computer. "Where is Mr. Stillman?"

She glanced at her watch. "If I had to guess, he's using the facilities. His coffee usually kicks in about now." She gestured down the hall. "I'm sure he'll be out in about ten minutes."

"We'll wait," Keller said.

Just ew. Ryley could just imagine the smell of that mixing with the heavy stench of oil.

Maybe she should have waited in the car.

Her day was getting better by the minute. She hobbled down the hallway, following the stink until she reached the bathroom. Using her crutch, she rapped on the door.

"Irene, the sky had better be falling," an angry voice yelled from the other side.

"Not the sky, but how about a car down a cliff?"

"Well, I never..." There was a rustle, and she heard the flush.

Hurrying back down the hall away from the potential stink, she braced herself for Larry to come out of the men's room.

He was as pissed as she thought he'd be, but didn't look anything like she'd expected. She'd expected balding and short. He was tall and heavy set like a bouncer. He could have snapped her in two with a single look.

It was a good thing she was flanked by a man with a badge, or it might have been her funeral they would have been attending next.

"Who the hell are you, and what is this about a car and a cliff?"

"One of your clients had her car worked on here, and as she drove it home, it killed her."

The man turned flustered. "You are wrong if you think it's because of my work. I've never had a complaint."

"I'd like to see Tessa Murphy's service order to see what work you performed on her vehicle," Keller said, flashing his badge.

The mechanic's eyes widened with a hint of fear.

"You got a warrant?" he asked.

"If you make us get a warrant, we'll be looking at more than that single work order. We'll be looking at all your books. How does that sound, Mr. Still-man?" Ryley said, trying her best to sound official.

"You got a badge, too?" Stillman asked.

Ryley gestured to Keller. "His is enough for both

of us. If you still don't want to help us, I'll be more than happy to go to the press."

"Really? Why would anyone even listen to you?"

"Wilson Foundation has connections, Mr. Stillman. I'm sure you don't want me to start pulling those threads. There's no telling how many imperfections I can find."

He snapped his mouth closed with a frown.

Ryley slipped her phone out of her pocket and used the hand in the sling to hold it while she pretended to dial. "Care to test me, Stillman?"

"All right, all right. I don't know what you think you're going to find, but I'll show you her ticket."

"And I want to see the surveillance videos from the day she picked up her car."

"Irene, pull the work order," Stillman demanded. "The security feed will be in my office, but I'm telling you now, you aren't going to see anything on it. That Murphy girl came to pick up her car and left without incident."

Ten minutes later, after watching the video, Ryley determined that his statement was a lie.

18

"Says here she had her tires rotated and new brakes installed. Nothing out of the ordinary," Keller said.

"Yeah, well, I think I've got something."

Keller pulled up a chair next to her. "What did you find?"

Ryley rewound that video and used her good leg to move the squeaky chair closer to the desk. "Tessa said a black truck ran her off the road."

"Do you see one following her?"

"Actually, I do. There is one that leaves behind her."

"Can you tell who's driving?"

"Not at this angle, but if I move back to when the truck arrived, I might we might be able to see a face." She moved the video further back in time and paused it when a man wearing a bouncer's shirt from Deadheads got out and headed into the shop to talk to one of the mechanics.

"Him. You can see him through the window. He gets out of the truck and talks to the mechanic for about five minutes and then gets in his truck and doesn't leave and doesn't move until Tessa picks up her car and pulls out. He follows minutes behind her."

"Stillman, I'm going to need access to download this security feed."

"Whatever. But you remember you said that if I cooperated that you wouldn't be back to look through my books or anything else?"

"One more thing and we'll be on our way," Keller said.

"What now?" Stillman asked.

"What is this mechanic's name?"

Stillman rounded the desk and slid the glasses from the top of his head to perch on his nose. He leaned in as if to get a better look. "That's Jimmy Petrella. He's been here for a couple of months. He's not here."

"Where can we find Jimmy?"

"Not sure. He doesn't have a physical address. The one he gave us was a friend's house, but I don't think he's staying there anymore. I think they had a falling-out."

Ryley pointed to the guy on the video that had been driving the black truck. "Was this the friend?"

"Yeah, it was. He's been in here a couple of times, but he's kind of standoffish and unfriendly."

"Is Jimmy coming in today?"

"I haven't seen him this morning," Stillman said, opening the office door. "Irene, when is Jimmy on the schedule next?"

"He'll be here in about an hour."

"You heard her," Stillman said.

"Great. We'll be back," Ryley said, shoving herself to stand up while Keller emailed himself the security feed from the online account.

She hobbled out of the shop and was heading toward the SUV when three men got out of a car across the parking lot. Two guys wearing Deadhead shirts went into the convenience store, and the last one, wearing a pizza shop uniform, splintered off and walked to the pizza shop. He knocked on the door, and a worker opened it and let him in.

None were the one who'd followed Tessa home.

She climbed into the SUV as Keller shoved her crutch in the backseat.

"What do you want to do now?"

"Take me to the police station."

"I never thought I'd hear you say that. Are you sure that's not the painkillers talking?"

She nodded and held in her evil smile. It was time for a little payback.

The ride across town to the sheriff's department held easy banter. Now that they shared the same secret, it was as if she could almost trust him. Almost believe they had the same goal. Almost.

They headed into the sheriff's department after a quick flash of the badge and a phone call. She led the way down the hall.

"That guy bother you, yet?" Keller asked with a head nod toward ghostly Marshall Boswell.

"Oh yeah, we have history. He keeps threatening to throw me in jail and toss away the key. He still thinks he runs this place and that his tarnished badge and the ghostly gun still work."

Keller grinned.

"He also thinks I'm a witch."

Keller chuckled. "You need to get better at pretending you don't see them. You'd probably have fewer personal hauntings."

"One would think," Ryley answered. Most of her hauntings were because she attended funerals. Funerals were a necessity, like breathing air. She'd found that out the hard way when her first apartment was across the street from a funeral parlor.

Crews looked up from his desk as she entered. His brows dipped.

"You look surprised to see me here," Ryley said as she hobbled into one of the chairs.

"You look like crap. What happened to you?" He turned his glare on Keller. "Did you let that happen?"

"Like anyone can tell her what to do." Keller shook his head and handed him the paperwork on Tessa's car.

"What's this?"

"Since you so wonderfully interrupted my last funeral, let's just say a new puppy followed me home."

"Oh." His eyes widened, and he picked up the paper, sat down, and read the work order. "Tessa Murphy."

"You need to check the forensics on the case. Her car didn't accidentally go into the ravine. You'll probably find evidence of foul play on her bumper from a black truck that was following her and sent her over the ledge.

"You believe this was intentional?"

"I don't believe it. I know it. Tessa said she was murdered."

"I'll see what I can dig up."

"No need. We already did it for you," Ryley said.

Keller picked up a business card and forwarded the security video to Crews. "If you'll pull up the video that I just sent you, we'll show you the potential suspect."

"I get why Ryley is here, but how did she talk you into this?"

"I need her to focus on Judge Henley's issue, and the only way she can do that is if we get answers for Tessa's family."

"That's where you come in," Ryley said as Crews opened his email and watched the video.

"That guy goes in and talks to the mechanic before Tessa shows up. He's seen waiting in the parking lot and leaves the same time she does after she gets her car. You'll need to question Jimmy, the mechanic."

"And the Deadhead bar bouncer," Ryley added. "I believe he's the one that pushed her into the ravine."

"Why do you believe that?"

"'Cause Tessa told me what type of truck was involved. He's the only one in the vicinity that follows her, and there was talk at the funeral about her and the Deadheads. Someone mentioned seeing her talking to one of those guys and leaving the bar.

Thought maybe she got involved with the wrong crowd. I'm sure security footage might be able to prove it one way or another."

"That bar isn't the normal place for the college crowd. I'll see what I can find out."

"Good," she said, trying to stand and grabbing her crutch. "If I have to keep doing your job, the sheriff is going to have to give me a badge, and just think of how much fun I could have with one of those."

"Yeah, right?" Crews chuckled. "I'll look into it and let you know what happens."

"Great, and after I deal with Henley's issue, then maybe my life can go back to normal," Ryley said as she hobbled back out the door.

Keller helped her into the SUV just as the first raindrop hit. He started the car and pulled out of the lot like he knew where he was going without directions. He probably did. She kept forgetting that he used to live in town.

"We going to Henley's house?"

"Nope," he answered. "Not yet. We have a pit stop to make."

She was watching the scenery pass by when her phone dinged with a message from Oscar.

Just checking on you to make sure you're alive.

She grinned and texted back. *No vacation for you yet, and Keller's still alive.*

That's always good to hear. Hiding bodies isn't as easy as one might think.

She chuckled and glanced up as Keller turned into the parking lot of the diner.

Got to run. Food is on the agenda. She hit Send.

He's a fast learner. You're unhelpful when you're hungry. Oscar sent a couple of emojis.

You know me best. Now go away. I need to get inside and order some pancakes before the bottom falls out.

Keller helped her out with the crutch and spotted her as she made her way into the diner. She took her normal booth, and Keller sat on the opposite side.

Maggie appeared with a frown. "You fall down some stairs or something?"

"Or something," she answered.

"Did a ghost do that to you?"

Ryley rubbed her sling-covered arm. "No, my own stupidity and lack of depth perception were involved."

Maggie poured them both a cup of coffee. "What do you guys want to eat?"

"Pancakes and bacon," she answered.

"Again? Aren't you tired of eating that?"

"Never." Ryley licked her lips as her stomach growled.

"You want the same thing?" Maggie asked Keller.

"Yes, please, and we're going to need the apple pie."

"Two slices are coming up," Maggie said and disappeared behind the counter.

"Oscar was right. You are learning." Ryley smiled as she tried her best to open the creamer pack and doctor up her coffee.

"I figured we should talk away from Henley's house, now that you know my secret."

"You know, you should have told me. If anyone would understand, it's me."

"I don't personally know you, and based on what Amanda used to tell me, she suggested that you weren't always on the up and up. Sometimes hanging with the wrong crowd."

Ryley shrugged. "I had a hard life, but I managed, and I'm stronger for it. You said it yourself. The decisions we make when we're younger don't define us. We grow from the experiences. We learn from them."

"Yeah, what have you learned?"

"That people lie. It's human nature. Not everyone has your best interests at heart. The world can be a mean place, but I've also seen it be beautiful, and not everyone is bad. There is a yin to the yang." Ryley took a sip of her coffee.

He slowly nodded and took a sip of his coffee. "And what about the spirits?"

"Are in death as they were in life. Some go into the light, and others have reasons to stick around, regardless of whether it's fear of their final destination or worry about loved ones. Nothing is textbook, and nothing is black and white."

His eyes gleamed with years of wisdom as he agreed.

"Let me ask you a question."

"Fire away," he said.

Maggie appeared with their pancakes, bacon, and pie. "Can I get you anything else?"

"I think we have everything we need." Ryley was quick to grab the syrup bottle.

Maggie scampered off to help an old man at the counter.

"What's your question?" Keller asked, patiently waiting and watching Ryley drown her breakfast.

"Lawmen mostly believe in evidence and what can be proved. How is it someone like you got into law enforcement?"

"Ada Mae Keller of the Manhattan Kellers comes

from a long line of law enforcement."

"You wouldn't know it by looking at her."

"She was a socialite through and through. The entire family is either law enforcement or helping to better society in some capacity, even going to the extreme of trying to fix the laws through politics."

"And can all the law enforcement men in your family do the thing you can do?"

"Most, and that's exactly why they joined. It's hard for normal law enforcement to fight what they can't see."

She flipped the lid on the syrup and passed him the bottle. "Where were you when I was five?"

"Probably in middle school playing football against your brother. He and I are close to the same age."

They took their time eating, questioning each other about their experiences and what it was like growing up. Ryley kept her stories on the side of law-abiding citizens. She had so many more stories that crossed the line. If he wasn't a cop, she might have shared them too.

Even though they weren't technically from the same side of the law, their family lineage shared a theme. His family was full of cops, and hers probably full of criminals.

19

Stopping in front of the broken-down fence at Henley's property had the butterflies in Ryley's stomach starting to flitter again. Ada Mae paced at the fence as Tessa stared on with anticipation. Stretch just looked annoyed.

"That's a motley crew if I've ever seen one," Keller said, coming to stand next to her.

"It bothers me they can't get in."

"Why is that? Because it's a boundary that you didn't personally make?"

"Yes," she said, folding her arms across her chest and turning an accusatory gaze on him. "You smudged my salt line at the farm. Didn't you?"

He grinned and shrugged. "I needed to see if

there were more than the dead teen and the stripper."

"Devious." She chuckled.

"I have my moments," he answered.

"So, what do you suppose is keeping our taga-longs off the property?"

"Maybe it's cursed," he said.

"Maybe there is a spell to keep the evil in."

"Or the good out," he offered. "One thing is for sure."

"What's that?"

"We may never know unless we can get the dead owner from the pictures to start talking."

"I forgot you probably saw him, too, that first day."

"And all the others," he added, pulling up the drive. He parked and guided her to the front door and helping her up the steps.

The house had the same repressed feeling the moment they stepped in the door. The things she'd left were in the exact same spot from when she'd grabbed her phone and gone to let Keller in the house. The apple pie sat untouched.

There was a depressing feeling in the house and the undeniable feeling that they were absolutely being watched.

Without voicing her opinion, she watched Keller slowly turn in place, his eyes as searching as hers had been.

"We aren't leaving," Ryley yelled, hoping her voice carried to the rafters.

Keller helped her to one of the couches and pulled the sheet off of it, helping her to sit down. "You take a load off while I go get rid of the pie before we add red ants to our problem."

She rested her head against the back of the couch, her gaze toward the dirty chandelier hanging above. Today it wasn't moving. Maybe because there was still light outside. Maybe these ghosts liked to be seen only at night or when they thought they could scare or kill.

A fast breeze flew by, blowing her hair. All she wanted to do was sage and kick these bastards out and salt the entrances, but if she didn't come up with a name, something to prove that she wasn't making stuff up, there was no telling what the unpredictable judge might do.

Keller returned and had the phone pressed to his ear. "I know. Yes, I said I know. I'm sorry. It can't be helped." His brows pinched as he hung up and re-pocketed his phone.

"Did you cancel your date?" she asked.

"No. It was just a coworker."

He didn't elaborate any more than that.

"Yeah, my bartender is going to be a bit pissed that I'm not going to be there to help tonight."

"You've obviously got money, hire a manager or more help."

"I've been meaning to."

"Maybe he'll feel sorry for you, seeing your bum foot and your sling."

"Hardly." Ryley sighed and shoved to stand, grabbing the crutch again. "He'll know it was my own fault. Or maybe he'll believe a ghost did it to me. It wouldn't be the first time one tried to do me in."

"Really?" Keller asked, taking some logs from the hearth and stacking them in the fireplace.

"Yep. As I said, I seem to bring out the best in everyone, dead or alive." She headed for the stairs.

"Where are you going?"

"See if I can get a damn name so we can cleanse the house. If we're lucky, we could be back to the farm by dinner time, and there won't be a need for whatever cavalry you called."

"Now, who's kidding herself?" he asked with an amused tone. "Oh, and by the way, that coworker just informed me that the cavalry is going to be delayed by a day. They had something unavoidable come up that they need to handle first."

"Your coworker is the cavalry?" Ryley paused near the top of the stairs. "How are they going to help, or have you forgotten that guns don't work on ghosts?"

"You wouldn't believe me if I told you," he said with a nudge of his chin as he grabbed more wood. "Happy hunting, and holler if you need me to come up there and carry you around."

"I've got it," she said from the landing. She headed down the opposite hallway, away from the master bedroom and the children's rooms.

With each step she took, the pressure in the hallway turned even more oppressive. Her heart raced as she gripped the crutch handle tighter, willing to use it as a weapon from rodents or anything else hiding in the space.

She turned the squeaky handle on the first door she came to and eased it open, greeted by stale air.

A bed sat between two side tables and across the room stood a dresser against the wall. The room, bath, and closet were all empty. There wasn't a single clue to tell her who had slept in that room.

She hobbled back out into the hallway and

farther down the hall, where the silence was all but deafening.

She opened the door, expecting to find another bedroom. She found a sort of dressing room instead.

A large floor-length mirror perched in front of a dais. Next to it stood a seamstress' mannequin, the torso covered with a lace wedding dress from decades ago. It was as though the house was frozen in history.

A shiver skirted her spine. Why hadn't Amanda removed it from the place? Surely something like a wedding dress held an emotional attachment. Women spent years looking forward to the day they'd say "I do." Some even turned into Bridezilla. Was that what they were dealing with here? Who would have left something like that behind?

Intricate lace eyelets were threaded through the fabric in the shape of a well-crafted floral design. A brooch nestled at the throat of the high-collared neck.

She felt like an intruder. A work table was across the room with a large array of threads, sharp scissors, and other supplies. Hanging on a metal rod were several other pieces of clothing. None from this century, and all with a waist that looked just about as big as Ryley's thigh.

They were all tasteful pieces.

She heard a loud creak coming from the hallway. She stepped out of the room and glanced in both directions. "Keller?"

"Yeah." She heard him call out from the direction of the stairs.

"Did you just open or shut a door?"

He appeared at the top of the stairs with the phone pressed to his ear again. He put his hand over the receiver. "No. You good?"

She nodded. "I'm fine. I think they're getting frisky."

Keller gave her a lopsided grin before it fell. "Yes, sir. I'm still here."

Keller disappeared down the stairs again, and she turned back toward the sound of the noise, wishing she had thought to bring her sage with her up the stairs.

She'd reached for the knob on the next door when she heard a whisper and felt a breeze coming from the hallway.

The last door at the end wasn't fully closed. She abandoned the door in front of her and hobbled to the partially opened door.

Pulling it open, she was met with the same creaky sound she'd heard before. A staircase rose in front of her, leading to what appeared to be an attic. A stench like no other wafted to her nose, making her want to slam the door closed.

No way was she running. If there was something up there, it was time to confront it.

20

Trepidation trembled in her fingers as they hovered near the light switch. Did she really want to go see what waited for her up the stairs?

She flicked the switch, bathing the stairway in flickering yellow light that looked as though it could give out and go dark again at any minute.

Some light was better than nothing. This time she'd brought her phone as her lifeline. She'd learned her lesson the last time the entities in the house bested them.

She jostled up one step and then two. An icy chill rushed against her flushed face and, with it, more of the stink from upstairs.

The sound of ghostly footsteps coming from above had her stilling once again.

"Whoever you are, I'm coming up. I'm not here to harm you." Yet. She hollered, "I just want to talk."

The walking stopped, replaced by a strange rustling sound as if someone or something was being dragged across the floor.

She fired off a text to Keller, not taking any chances. *Headed into the creepy attic to take a look-see.*

"The sooner we have this conversation, the quicker the other guy and I will be gone," she lied.

She moved again, slowly, watching as shadows darted by, blocking out the light, slowly, methodically, trying mentally to prepare for who or whatever might rush her from above.

She swallowed hard and stepped into the room. The attic was filled with storage. Things that were long forgotten, similar to the ghosts hiding up there.

"Who's up here with me?" she asked, facing the window that pointed to the parking below.

A rustling sound from behind had her spinning as best she could toward the noise, looking for the culprit. The light momentarily flickered again.

"Was it you that locked us out?" Ryley asked as her gaze touched everything in sight, looking for any movement. "That was kind of smart. You must be pretty strong to shut doors and turn locks. Have you been dead for a while?"

The only answer she got was from the flickering bulb overhead again.

"This place needs an electrician, unless that's you stealing the power." Ryley waited. "If you talk to me, I'll be able to hear you," she said, moving across the room with her hand over her nose, trying hard to cover the stench.

She reached for some dusty boxes and opened the one on top to find linens. As she was about to jostle it to the side to see what was in the next one, she got a glimpse of something on the floor behind it. She shoved the box out of the way.

On the floor lay a newspaper with a dead featherless bird, its black feathers scattered around it. Next to it was a dead rat carcass whose insides were hanging out.

She took an unconscious step back into what felt like an actual body.

"Get out!" a younger male voice screamed in her ear. The frigid chill settled in her bones.

A hard pressure pushed at the back of her knee, making it give out and knocking her to the floor. What or whoever they were dealing with was undoubtedly strong.

"Tell me your name and I'll leave you alone for the night."

Silence.

"What's the matter? Did you use all your energy?" Ryley asked.

More silence.

"Guess maybe I'll bring my bed up here for the night. Maybe I'll mess with all this stuff. Was some of it yours?"

The lightbulb flickered once again before the bulb shattered, raining down onto the floor. The attic door slammed.

Territorial. Now she was getting somewhere.

She hobbled toward the stairs to find the door below was now shut.

She pulled out her phone and dialed Keller, only for it to go straight to voicemail. So, she texted instead.

I'm in the attic. I pissed off a ghost, and it slammed the door and blew the bulb. If you come looking for me, don't get locked up here, too.

"I just warned my friend about you, so we both don't get stuck up here. I'm guessing you're ready to talk since you blocked my exit and don't want me to go?"

A shadow on the far wall dashed across the room, blocking the light from the only window.

"Haven't you missed talking to people? I can hear

you. I heard you yell at me to leave," Ryley said, jostling to one of the boxes near the window, keeping the darkness in front of her. She sat on top of the box.

"If you wanted me to leave, then why did you shut the door? You obviously didn't think that one through," she said with a sigh, agitated that she wasn't getting any more responses.

"Did you kill the animals?"

No response.

The repressed feeling that she'd gotten coming up the stairs vanished and was replaced by emptiness. She was alone.

"Perfect."

Hearing a muffled voice, she turned to the window to find Keller outside, talking loudly and adamantly on the phone.

Pulling out her phone, she shined it around the area, reading the boxes and peeking inside to see that most of it was the normal junk people stash in their attics—clothes, linens, Christmas decorations, a couple of photo albums. There were family heirlooms and furniture that looked older than the house. Memories that probably once meant something to people, but now had no one alive to appreciate them.

She hobbled for the stairs and inched down, one by one, with a hand on the railing in anticipation of the ghost coming back and trying to finish the job. A forced tumble down these stairs might just break her neck.

She reached the bottom without incident and turned the handle.

Unlocked. A sigh of relief passed her lips as she stepped back out into the hallway.

A different scent smacked her in the nose the closer she got to the stairs leading downstairs. Smoke made her cough as another fear took hold.

Flames danced in the fireplace, but blankets from the cot had started to spark.

She hobbled down the stairs with her hand on the rail, catching herself from falling in her haste. She threw the front door open, hurrying out of the house.

"Fire," she yelled out, coughing and bending over.

Keller spun in her direction. His feet were already moving. "Where?"

She gestured inside. "The fireplace and cot."

He glanced inside before running to the back of the SUV and returning with a fire extinguisher. He rushed back inside to battle the blaze.

Ada Mae Keller, Stretch, and Tessa watched helplessly from the gate.

"Help him!" Ada Mae yelled out.

"No," Stretch growled. "Then she'll die too."

Tessa remained quiet and stared on like the wind in her sails was slowly leaking.

Ryley moved back inside the door to find everything from the fireplace to the cot engulfed in white foam. The entire fire was extinguished.

"What did you do?" Keller asked, moving their things farther away from the chaos.

"Me?" She gawked. "Oh no, no, no. This isn't on me. I was upstairs in the attic. Don't you read your texts? I was just coming down and smelled the smoke."

"Well, I didn't do it," Keller said. "When I walked out, the flame was dying down and it was contained in the fireplace."

"Must have been the ghost that told me to get out. I provoked him, telling him I was going to sleep up in the attic."

Keller's eyes flashed. "And you came down to find the cot on fire? Do you know who it is yet?"

"Nope, but they've mastered energy manipulation; blew a bulb, shut the attic door, hit my locked knee from behind."

"Did you fall?"

"Not this time. And they screamed at me to leave. The next thing I knew, I was alone up there. The energy had shifted." She gestured to the hearth. "Now I know why. Seems he found something more destructive to do. We need to get a name so we can sage this bastard out once and for all."

"Looks like we're on our own until tomorrow. My team was delayed." He moved to his bag and unzipped it, pulling out a video camera and two voice recorders. "They suggested we document what we can until they get here."

Keller walked over to her and showed her where the on switch was on the device before turning it off and slipping the device into her sling. "Let me get this on video, and we can let the place air out before we really go piss these spirits off."

"How do you suppose we do that?"

Keller grinned. "How much do you like people poking in your belongings?"

"Not at all."

"Yeah, well, it seems things increased when you were in the attic. They must have wanted you out for a reason. How about we go poke that bear with a sharper stick?"

She nodded. Hopefully, they didn't get burned in

the process. She wasn't sure she'd survive a fall from the third floor.

"As long as there is no fire and we have another way out, I'm game. We need to get this done." Before it sent her back to the hospital or, worse, home in a body bag.

21

Ryley's phone rang as she glanced at the caller ID. "It's just Oscar. I'm going to go out on the porch to get some fresh air."

He nodded.

She hobbled out and sat before answering her phone.

"What's wrong?" Oscar growled. "Tell me you're not in trouble again."

"What are you talking about?"

"I'm going to venture a guess that Stretch isn't with you?"

Ryley lifted her gaze to the gate to find the ghost gone. "Looks like she left."

"That's because she's here. I got out of the

shower, and your name was written in the condensation on the mirror."

Ryley sighed. "We had a little situation."

"I thought she couldn't get past the gate," Oscar asked with confusion clouding his voice.

"She can't. I guess it freaked her out when I came out of the house yelling, 'Fire!'. She didn't want me to go back in."

"Tell me you didn't." Oscar paused. "Did you call the fire department?"

"It was a small fire. Keller contained it with a fire extinguisher."

"Glad one of you was prepared."

"It's a long story, but we're about to air out the smoke and then go back in to rile them up again."

"Ryley…"

"I know. I'll be careful."

"Well, if it's any consolation, I found someone from the family you can talk to."

"Really?" Ryley perked up, feeling a jolt of refreshed energy. "I thought they were all dead."

"The blood relatives are. The child they sent back to the orphanage is still alive."

Oh, Good Lord. "What are we looking at? Son of Satan? Might explain the ritualistic sacrificed dead animals in the attic."

"Dead animals?" Keller asked, coming out onto the porch.

She covered the phone's receiver. "Mutilated bird and dead rat."

Keller's mouth parted, and then he snapped it closed. "You stay here."

"Not a problem," she said, waving as he left.

"I'm not even going to ask," Oscar said, "As for Son of Satan, that would be a no, and she doesn't look like his daughter either."

"I bet you had to kick a few rocks to find out that information."

"You're right. They adopted two kids, a brother and a sister. Kept the boy and sent the girl back. I haven't determined why yet, but I can tell you that she lives across town."

"Text me the address, and Keller and I will go see what we can find out. Surely the girl will have some knowledge of what went on here. Something tells me what we're looking for isn't going to be in any of the history books."

"Stay vigilant, Ryley. Mishaps have happened twice while you were on the property. This spirit seems a bit more determined to silence you than most others."

More determined. Not hardly. There were plenty

of other encounters involving other ghosts and people that she hadn't told Oscar about. Plenty that he still didn't know, and she planned to keep it that way.

"I'll be fine. I've got backup, and this time he can actually see the threats."

Keller appeared on the porch and gestured inside with his thumb.

"I've got to go. Text me the girl's address and the name of the orphanage. Someone has to know something."

"You've got it," Oscar said, disconnecting the call.

"Did you touch the animals?" Keller asked.

"Uh, that would be a hell no. No way am I getting swine flu or whatever bad juju those suckers succumbed to."

"Good. I'll send them back to forensics to see if I can find a cause of death."

"A serial killer did that. Haven't you ever learned anything from the FBI? I thought that was standard procedure for serial killers. At a young age, they start with small animals and then move on to bigger prey."

"Some analysts might say that, but we're not dealing with normal circumstances here. For all we know, some black magic could have been going on. Might explain the darker entity in the house."

"Black magic isn't in my wheelhouse," she admitted, unsure what to do if that was the case. Her phone beeped with the address. "Oscar told me a story while you were looking at the dead things. How about I fill you in on the way to find out what really happened here?"

"You found someone who might know."

"Maybe, although I'm a bit leery of why the family kept her sibling and returned her to the children's home. I have no idea what we'll be walking into."

And with their luck, she felt like they had better be prepared for just about anything.

22

Ryley used the GPS on her phone to point the direction across town and out to the suburbs.

"Looks like Shelby McNally has done okay for herself after growing up in an orphanage," Keller said as he parked at the curb where Ryley pointed.

"You'd be surprised at what desperate people can do," Ryley said, waiting and watching the house in question. Most of the houses on the street had palm trees planted in the yard as if that were a requirement or something the homeowners' association insisted on. Where the other driveways had two cars parked nearby with bikes and toys inside the safety of a fence, Shelby's house was different.

It was well past dinner time. The other houses on the street had movement behind their curtains.

Families were sitting down for dinner, the glares from the TV lighting the houses. Shelby's house was dark. Across the street, a man stood outside smoking a cigarette, talking to a neighbor, who was drinking a beer.

Shelby's house was missing life. Dark behind the curtains. No cars in the driveway. No toys on the meticulously cut lawn. Nothing to suggest anyone even lived there.

"Doesn't look like she's home yet. Any idea where she works?"

"She's a nurse. Her shift ended thirty minutes ago. Maybe she's got a favorite patient that she's giving a sponge bath," Ryley answered, giving information from the text Oscar had sent earlier.

"Or maybe she's like normal people and had to stop by the store. You want to wait?"

She wanted to do more than that, like sneak into the house and dig into secrets Shelby might not want to share, but not with neighbors already looking on curiously in their direction.

"You think they're going to call the law on us?" Ryley asked.

"It doesn't matter if they do," Keller said, looking at the neighbors. "You want me to go flash my badge?"

"Nah. Someone might call Shelby and tell her not to come home." Ryley turned back to the house in question to study it some more.

"You say that like you're speaking from experience."

She'd always been told never to judge a book by its cover. Ryley was a prime example of why. She might have worked as a bartender and moved around from apartment to apartment most of her life, but no one would have ever been able to tell that she had her fair share of secrets, that there was nothing remotely normal about her.

There never would be. The moon had lifted into the sky as they sat there. The neighbors had finally stepped back inside. A couple was walking their dog down the street.

"Maybe we should go," he offered, turning the ignition.

Before she could even answer, a four-door sedan turned into the driveway.

A woman with shoulder-length blond hair stepped out wearing hospital scrubs, an ID hanging around her neck. She opened the backseat door and grabbed a single grocery bag.

"You win. She's got a grocery bag," Ryley said.

Keller opened his door, and Ryley followed. He

waited for her on the sidewalk as they made their way up the driveway.

"Excuse me, are you Shelby McNally?"

She turned abruptly, as if they'd startled her.

"Who wants to know?" Shelby asked.

Keller flashed his badge. "I'm Special Agent Roger Keller, and this is Ryley St. James. Can you spare a moment to talk to us?"

She took his badge and frowned. A shot of unease crossed her eyes before she quickly covered it and handed it back. She jostled her bag on her hip and headed for the door.

"Here, let me help you with that," Keller said, relieving Shelby of the bag while she unlocked the door and flicked on the light.

He followed her to the kitchen and put the bag down on the counter.

"What's this about?"

"It's about the Batemans."

"Wow. I haven't heard that name in a long time," she said, unpacking her groceries and putting them away before grabbing a beer from the fridge. "Whatever they claimed I did, they're lying."

"They haven't claimed anything. They're all dead."

She sputtered on her beer. "All of them? Are you sure?"

"Yes. We're sure."

"Hot damn." Shelby grinned. "This calls for the good stuff."

"I'm guessing you didn't like them much," Ryley asked as she teetered on the crutch.

"Hell no. They practically ruined my life," the woman said, gesturing to a kitchen chair. "You should sit before you fall over."

Keller pulled out a chair, and Ryley sat.

"Who else wants champagne?" she asked.

"I'm on the clock," Keller said.

"I'm on painkillers, and I'm afraid it would put me to sleep when I have to stay up the rest of the night."

"Why is that?" Shelby asked. "You work the midnight shift or something?"

"Something like that," Ryley answered.

"More for me." Shelby popped the cork on the champagne and poured a generous amount into a travel sized cup. She sipped, crinkling her nose as she pulled it away.

"If you don't mind me asking, how did they ruin your life?" Keller asked with a tilt of his head as if he were studying her.

"They kept me from my brother when they sent me back to the orphanage. Granted, that wasn't a bad thing. Living in that house was a horror in itself, but there's a stigma attached to orphans that get sent back. People think we're bad seeds, unruly and unlovable."

"Was that the case with you?"

"I had my moments, but I eventually aged out. Worked my way through nursing school. Ate a lot of noodles and rice. It was tough, but I put in the time and survived."

"Does it make you angry that you didn't have the same comforts that your brother did?"

Shelby's eyes narrowed. "Is that what this is about? Did you find Ethan?"

Keller shared a confused look with Ryley. "Find him? Is he lost? I thought he was dead like the rest of the family."

Her shoulders sagged. "I used to call him, you know. They let me talk to him most of the time. He was my brother, after all." She shrugged. "I think they just did that to appease me so that I wouldn't cause any trouble. On his sixteenth birthday, I called and they told me he was unavailable. A week later, they told me he didn't want to talk to me. Two weeks later, when I threatened to go public about my experience at their house if they didn't let me talk to him, they finally told me that he ran away."

"Did they say why he ran away?"

"Just that he didn't like their rules."

"And you believed them?"

She took another long sip from her cup. "Yes, I could see that. I knew it was a matter of time before one of them had enough."

"In the time that he lived there, did you ever go visit?"

"No, I wasn't allowed to go back. Not after the incident."

"The incident that you threatened to go public with?" Keller asked.

Shelby slowly lowered her cup. "I'm not allowed to talk about it."

"They're all dead. What does it matter?" Ryley asked.

Hesitation flickered in Shelby's eyes, and she grabbed her purse and pulled out a pack of cigarettes. She offered each of them one, but they declined.

She lit up and took a drag, blowing out the smoke before she continued.

"My last night there before they returned me, they had put me to bed, and it was a rule that we weren't allowed to leave our rooms at night, to the point they'd lock our doors."

"Let me guess. Claustrophobia or rule breaker?"

"Both, I guess." She shrugged. "I was trying to be good. Ethan liked it there. He liked his room and not having to share one with a bunch of boys. He wanted us to stay. So, I tried." Sadness flicked in her eyes as if the memory were replaying fresh in her mind.

"But you didn't stay, did you?" Keller asked, prodding her on.

She shook her head. "My room had a balcony that wrapped around the back of the house. It was hot in my room, so I opened the door to let a breeze in. I was about to climb back into bed when I heard a scream. It froze me on the spot. You have to understand. I was a little girl in a foreign house with adults I didn't trust."

"So, you went to search for the source of the scream?" Keller asked.

23

Shelby downed the rest of her champagne, wiped her mouth with the back of her hand, and took another drag of her cigarette. "Yeah. I did."

She rubbed at her face and let out a hesitant sigh, like this was a subject she hadn't broached in years.

"My room was right next door to Ethan's room. I went out on the balcony and tiptoed in search of whatever room the scream had come from. Ethan's room was empty."

"I bet that worried you," Ryley said. "It would if it was my brother."

Only if it had happened to Ryley, her brother, Tuck wouldn't have done that. He'd done his fair share of bursting into her room with a baseball bat to beat the closet monsters and ghosts that scared her growing up. If it hadn't been for her brother, she wouldn't be the woman she was today.

"Freaked me out. His door was open. So, I went in the other direction toward Mr. and Mrs. Bateman's room."

"And?" Keller asked.

"And nothing. The room was dark too, so I went back to my room, only when I got back, my door was closed, and it was locked. It was cold out that night. I can remember it like it was yesterday."

"That doesn't explain why they sent you back. What did you see?" Ryley prodded. "You can tell us."

Her eyes flickered to Keller, and another slip of hesitation crossed her gaze.

"Something illegal?" Ryley asked. "It's okay. They're all deceased. You can't get them in trouble."

"I was huddled on the porch trying to stay warm while waiting for my brother to come back to his room so he could let me back in. That way, I could sneak into my room."

She rubbed at her temple.

"Shelby, what happened next?" Ryley prodded.

"I shouldn't…"

"Shelby, tell me what happened," Keller said in his most authoritative tone.

"It happened again."

"What happened again?" Ryley asked.

"The scream. Only this time, I knew where it came from." She looked between them both, almost as if she was afraid to say so. "The attic."

"Okay, what was happening in the attic?"

"It wasn't the scream that scared me. Well, it was, but not entirely. It was the woman's death-curdling scream as she fell from the attic window."

"Did she jump, or did something else happen?" Keller asked.

"It startled me. I leaned over the railing to the woman below. Blood was coming out of her mouth and behind her head. So, I looked up to see where she'd come from."

"And what did you see?"

"Mr. Bateman and my brother were staring back at me."

"Well, hell," Ryley whispered, more to herself than to Shelby. "You saw a murder, and you didn't think to tell someone?"

"I couldn't. I mean they said no one would believe me. They said that the woman jumped. Mr. Bateman said if I tried to say she was murdered that they'd just blame it on Ethan. So, I was damned if I did and damned if I didn't."

"You witnessed a crime, and you didn't come forward."

"I was a stupid kid and I don't know if that woman jumped. She could have, for all I know. All I do know is that Ethan was up there, too. He was just a scared kid. I had to protect him."

"He's your brother. It's what sisters do," Ryley said.

Shelby met her gaze. "Exactly."

"Can you describe the woman?"

"I can do better than that. I can tell you, her name."

"What's that?"

"Susan Ramsey."

"You're sure that was her name? How do you know? Had they introduced you to her, or was she on the staff there?"

Shelby raised her brow in contempt. "Earlier that day, they'd introduced me to her. They said she wasn't just the maid; she was my mother."

24

"You witnessed your mother's death?" Ryley's eyes widened in disbelief.

"Murder. You witnessed your mother's murder," Keller corrected and leaned forward. "Didn't you want justice for her? Weren't you scared to leave your brother alone in that environment?"

The light in her eyes dimmed. "When I saw my brother in the attic window looking down"—she paused— "he was smiling. They both were. The next thing I know, Mr. Bateman is driving me back to the orphanage, and he's threatening me the entire way. Tells me if I talk, he'll kill both my brother and me and tell the cops that my brother pushed my mom out the window."

"Wow," Ryley said, unsure of what else to say. "Some people really do suck."

"Anyway, I thought you were here to tell me that you found Ethan. Don't get me wrong, I'm thrilled the old man is dead, but I'm still missing my brother."

"Had you filed a missing person report?" she asked.

"No. The Batemans told me they had filed it. They said they had connections."

"They didn't. Not in anything I've seen," Keller said.

"Yeah, well, you didn't see Ethan's face. The joy he took in seeing her dead body. When he came back to the room, he was all excited about it. Told me about how we could finally move past her betrayal. How she got what she deserved for abandoning us. Something changed between us that day. I cried until I was out of tears, and my brother was acting as if he had the best birthday present ever."

"You're his family. You should still file a report."

"After years growing up at the Batemans', I'm not sure I want to see how he turned out."

That was harsh but totally understandable. There was no telling how Ryley would have turned out if she'd been made to live with her father instead of running away with her mom and brother. A life of anger, lies, and betrayal would have ruined her for the rest of her life.

"How did Mr. Bateman die?" Shelby asked.

"He died of a heart attack," Keller said, glancing at her ID. "At your hospital. I'm surprised you didn't know."

She shrugged. "I don't know everyone that comes and goes from the hospital. I might not even have been working when it happened." She rose from the table and moved back into the kitchen. "If you don't have any more questions, I need to start dinner. I have an early shift tomorrow."

"Sure." Ryley grabbed the crutch and hobbled toward the door. "We appreciate your help."

"No problem," Shelby called out.

"One more thing." Keller paused at the door. "In the little time you were there, did you notice anything odd?"

"Odder than the owners?" she asked.

"Cold spots. Strange noises in the night. Stuff moving."

She shook her head and pressed her lips together. "Can't say I did. Well, nothing but that first scream that got me locked on the balcony."

He gave a slow nod. "And did you ever figure out who locked the door?"

"No." Shelby started pulling out ingredients. The conversation was over.

"Have a good evening, Ms. McNally."

"Sorry I couldn't be of more help, Special Agent Keller. I wouldn't be totally surprised if you find dead bodies all over that place. I don't think my mom was the first death on the property."

"What makes you say that?" Keller asked.

She shrugged with a knowing look like she knew more. "Just a hunch. I mean, what type of sicko would orchestrate all that and kill my mom? That took planning. Like he had to have known about me, my brother, and my mother before ever bringing us home. It's no coincidence. I think he was sadistic."

"Something we need to look into," Keller said, turning back to Shelby. "Thanks for your time."

Keller helped Ryley into the car and started the ignition. They sat in silence, digesting everything they had just learned.

"It's not a coincidence." Ryley offered.

"How do you think Bateman made the connection between all of them?"

"Maybe the mom mentioned it to someone at work, and one of the Batemans overheard her.

Maybe she pissed him off, turning down his advances. Maybe it was revenge."

"We don't even have a dead body yet. Maybe we should let the facts or the ghosts tell us what happened."

She grinned and turned to him. "If it's her spirit haunting the property, then find me a body and I can tell you what happened. As an added bonus, I can move her along too."

His brows pinched. "How is that? Do you have a degree in forensics?"

"I'm gifted in more ways than one. If the spirit is around, I can do psychometry with bones. It will show me their last moments before I send them into the light."

He frowned and started the ignition. "What do you mean, you can send them into the light?"

"I touch their bones, I see the secrets of their last moments, and then it's like they have no choice but to move on. I'm kind of like a catalyst that sends them packing."

"How?"

She shrugged. "I have no idea. It's not like I have an instruction manual or anything."

"I'm guessing not many people know that secret about you?"

"No, and I'd like to keep it that way."

"Is that why you go to funerals?"

"If the spirits move on, there are less sleepless nights for me."

"Interesting. I have a few dead bodies I might one day like you to touch."

Her eyes flashed in intrigue. "That sounds like an interesting story."

"It is." He grinned. They drove in silence for a few minutes. "You realize we're probably dealing with more than one ghost. We did get locked out on the balcony like Shelby."

"And up in the attic. When we first pulled up to the place, I saw more than one ghost," she said, turning in his direction.

"I did too." He put the car in drive. "I'll call the sheriff and tell him we're going to need cadaver dogs, and I'm going to have to do a deeper dive on the employees to see if I can find any record of Shelby's mother or any others that went missing or just disappeared."

"Something tells me that you won't find anything. Judging by the sound of things, the family that lived there was connected. Connected enough to get rid of a maid without anyone asking questions. There is no telling how many others," Ryley said.

As he drove back toward the property, her stomach tightened with each street they passed. Ghosts were one thing. Darker entities and serial-killing ghosts were a whole other ball game.

"No one is going to believe Shelby that any of that actually happened, though I seriously doubt she'll ever repeat the story."

Ryley pulled out the recorder tucked in her sling and waved it. "I made sure this story won't die with us."

"Clever." He grinned.

Stretch appeared in the backseat. *"I think this one might be a keeper. At least he can see us."*

"Sorry." He turned to Ryley. "No offense, but I'm already interested in someone else, and I have no desire to move back to this town."

"I don't blame you, and no offense taken."

"I don't think you should go back into that house. Not until you figure out a way to remove the boundaries that are keeping us out. You need us inside to help you. Ada Mae agrees with me." Stretch sighed as if she actually had a breath in her ghostly body, leaning forward in the backseat like a kid getting a first glimpse at an amusement park out the front window.

"We have it under control. I'm watching Ryley's back, and she's watching mine," Keller said. "You can tell my grandmother that, too."

"It's refreshing to have someone that can see the same things as I can. Most times, I have to convince people I'm not crazy," Ryley said, turning her attention toward the passing houses.

"Ryley, don't go back in," Stretch begged.

"I'll be fine," Ryley answered, turning toward the backseat. "But you know how you can help me?"

"How?"

"Try to talk Tessa into moving on. I talked to her sister. She knows the danger, and Crews is looking into the case. There's nothing more she can do here. She needs to move on."

Stretch held her gaze as if debating her answer. *"I'll try, but don't expect miracles. That girl's as stubborn as you."*

Stretch vanished as Keller turned into the drive, hitting the brakes.

"We didn't magically close the gate when we left, did we?"

"Maybe the ghosts did and hoped we weren't returning," she answered.

He opened the gate, slowly drove through the driveway, and parked in front of the house. Pulling out his gun, he checked the clip before shoving it back inside.

"Wait here."

"You don't have to tell me twice," she said as he got out. She locked the doors behind him. Her gaze darted to all the windows above, scanning for whatever signs of a threat she could find, living or dead.

25

Only now, the old man with the graying hair and hard face from the first time she'd arrived at the house was staring down from the window above.

Judging by the pictures she'd seen of the previous family; he wasn't even the same Bateman who had killed Shelby's mother. Darkness surrounded him; unlike anything she'd seen before.

Within seconds, he vanished from sight.

Ryley eased her window slightly down to hear shouts, gunshots, or whatever else might transpire inside.

When nothing came, and Keller remained gone for longer than ten minutes, she decided enough was enough.

Getting out of the car, she hobbled up the steps

and inside, over to where her bag still lay on the floor.

She unzipped the bag to find her things still inside. Pulling out her Taser, she turned it on and set on the floor, unwrapping her foot and putting on one of her socks.

Testing the pressure on her foot, she took one tentative step and then two, happy that she could apply a little pressure, even though the mass was still swollen. She'd be able to move quicker this way. Quieter.

She limped throughout the living room and kitchen to find everything exactly how they'd left it.

Going to the stairs, she kept her back to the wall, breathing through the discomfort of her foot as she made her way to the next level.

The landing was empty.

She peeked around the corner in the direction of the attic, expecting to hear or see something.

Nothing

A rustling noise came from the direction of the master suite. She was gingerly making her way in that direction when the light above flickered, making the hair on her arms stand on end.

"Keller," she whispered, hoping that she wasn't outing them both.

Something felt off in the energy of the house.

"Ryley, I told you to stay in the car," Keller growled, coming out of the room. "There's no one up here."

Ryley glanced at the attic door. "Have you looked up there?"

"Nope. That's the next stop." He glanced at her sock. "Where is your crutch and your bandage?"

"I ditched it. I needed to be mobile in case you needed me."

"When we're done, I'll go get you some ice, and you can put your foot up."

"I'll be all right." Ryley gestured toward the other end of the house. "How about we finish this?"

He moved past her. "Stay behind me."

She saluted him with her Taser and slowly followed behind, ignoring the throbbing pain in her foot.

He pulled open the door and hollered up the stairs.

"FBI. Show yourself and keep your hands where I can see them."

He waited patiently, only no answer came.

"Time's up," Ryley called out. She went to walk around him, and he pulled her back, taking the lead.

Keller flicked the light, only for nothing to happen.

"It blew," she reminded him.

He continued up the stairs and into the attic, pointing his gun and turning in each direction as he checked the room.

"It's clear," he called out.

She moved to the window and was about to open it when Keller stopped her. "This is a crime scene. There might still be prints from Ethan or Shelby's mom."

"Even if fingerprints are still here, it wouldn't matter, considering they lived here." She peered out at the yard below, imagining what a fall from that height might be like.

"Humor me."

"She was probably scared to death," Ryley whispered.

"I'm sure she was," Keller said. "Come on, let's get you back downstairs. We need to discuss sleeping arrangements. I think for the night, we need to be in the same room."

"Convenient ploy. I thought you were interested in someone else," Ryley teased.

"Seriously. Just for the night, until the team gets here; that way, I'm nearby if another ghost tries to hurt you," Keller said, plodding down the hall and checking the rooms again as he passed. "I'll make us a place to sleep in the living room."

"Or...we can go back to the farm and come back with fresh eyes in the morning and with a cadaver dog."

Darkness had fallen hours ago. Dinner was long past. She could read the debate in his eyes. If they stayed, they could try and deal with the spirits quicker and figure things out. If they left, it would be safer. She knew exactly what he was thinking because she was thinking it, too.

"One more day shouldn't hurt. Maybe by then we'll find some bones, and my team will be here to help. We'll be in a much better, safer position in the morning."

A cool breeze flitted across her face as he grabbed both of their bags and headed to the door. "It's the smart thing to do."

She glanced once more at the stairs above, feeling the heaviness of someone watching them. Probably waiting for them to leave or upset that they wouldn't get the chance to hurt them again. Either way, there would be more targets the next day, and she could be stealthier in her approach.

She was gearing up for her fight with the afterlife.

The ride to the farm was much lighter. The heaviness from the evening had slowly started to dissipate. Oscar was waiting for them. They all settled in the living room, Ryley with her foot propped up and packed with ice. Keller was across the room, laughing at a joke Oscar had told him.

Ringwald jumped up on the couch next to Ryley and rested his snout on her lap. She stroked his furry head with her good hand. Only hours ago, she was debating whether to trust Keller with the truth, and now he knew everything. Well, what she was willing to divulge.

Her phone rang, and she glanced at the caller ID to find Tucker's name popping up.

"Hey, Tuck," she answered. "Is everything okay?"

"I should be asking you the same thing," Tucker said.

"I'm fine. We're at the farm."

"Making any progress on Henley's house?"

"Getting there," she answered.

"So, the place is haunted?"

"Yeah, it is. I just don't have the name for him yet, or more information on what happened to Amanda. We're working on it."

There was a deep tension and hesitation on Tucker's end. She could feel it as if she were in the room sitting next to him.

"What's wrong?" she asked, moving the ice and dropping her foot to the ground. She rose and started to limp out of the room and into the kitchen.

"Seems Jennings' case has been postponed."

"What? Why?" Ryley growled. "It's open and shut. He isn't the killer."

"Apparently there is some question regarding procedure."

Ryley frowned and narrowed her eyes, looking out into the darkness of the backyard. "Procedure as in your sister can talk to ghosts?"

"He hasn't come out and said that, but I think that's where it's headed. The judge postponed the hearing until Monday, while he goes through the evidence."

"You mean I have until Monday to get Judge Henley some answers?"

"Ryley, I'd never ask…"

"You didn't have to, Tuck. Come hell or high water, I'll have the ghost evicted and a name for Judge Henley. I won't let the fact that I helped you hurt your case. Jennings has served enough time behind bars. He needs to be released so the police can start looking for the actual killer."

"Ryley, we shouldn't have to give in to blackmail in order to see justice."

In a perfect world, they wouldn't. "It's fine. Keller and I already have a plan. He has a team coming in, and he's getting cadaver dogs for the property. I'll get you some answers. Just give me the rest of the weekend."

"Thanks, Ryley. I owe you one."

"And I'll collect." She grinned.

"You always do." He chuckled. They talked for a bit longer, catching up on everything that had happened over the last couple of days. He was surprised to find out about Shelby.

"You have Logan Bane looking into things as well?"

"I'm sure Oscar has everyone pulling strings on this one. The stakes are high, not just for you and your case but for Oscar's well-being too. If the Judge decides I conned my way into Wilson's will, it could be reversed and go to that despicable cousin."

One way or another, she'd get to the bottom of things even if she had to start digging up graves and touching bones. She was going to get answers from these ghosts and this family, or she'd die trying.

"Your brother?" Oscar asked as he entered with empty beer bottles. He tossed them into the trash and grabbed two more.

"Yeah, he's worried about his case."

"I have all our resources looking into it. Is there anything else I can do to help?" Oscar asked. "I've offered to help Kent at the bar tomorrow to cover your shift, but you've got me until then. Just tell me what you need."

Ryley shrugged. "I don't know what I need. Shelby's mom was killed on the property. She witnessed it. She thinks there were probably more. Hell, they might have even killed her brother, Ethan."

"He turned up missing?" Oscar asked.

"Yeah, the Batemans claimed that they reported it to the police, so Shelby didn't. If he is dead, then he slipped through the cracks."

"I'll have Bane look into it. He's a good detective and tracker."

She knew firsthand. "One of the best. If Ethan is alive, I'm sure Bane will find him."

One way or another, she was going to see his case through if she had to lie, cheat, and steal to deal with the blackmail hanging over all of their heads.

26

Morning came early, and with it came the feeling of spirits watching her sleep. She rolled over and opened her eyes, rubbing at the sleep.

"My room is off-limits," Ryley said, sitting up.

Ada Mae Keller of the Manhattan Kellers was poised in a chair across the room, watching her.

"You aren't what I expected." Her disapproving voice, however quiet, was filled with contempt. *"I thought you'd be helpful."*

"What the hell do you think I've been doing?" Ryley asked with a frown.

"Getting yourself hurt. You're not going to be any good at watching his back if you're dead."

"Listen here, lady, I don't come from a long line of cops and socialites with clout in my family like he does, but I can tell you I come from a long line of criminals. I know how their minds work."

Ada Mae stared on disapprovingly.

"If you haven't noticed, he's not the one getting hurt. He won't die because of this case."

Ada Mae's disapproving glare started to give way. *"If what you say is true about your background, then you aren't right for him, either."*

"Good lord, lady. Let the man breathe. Let him live. Let him make a million mistakes if he has to. That way, he can appreciate things when they turn good. You can't control his life, and if you keep trying to, then he'll be missing out on all the lessons he was supposed to learn in this lifetime. Do you want that?"

"The girl he's dating isn't the right woman for him, either. I don't care what he believes. He's wrong." Ada Mae disappeared from sight.

Moments later, while Ryley was in the shower, Stretch appeared sitting on the bathroom sink. The scent of her expensive perfume was always the first warning. The perfume had started as a gift from one of the guys at the strip club who used to come see her dance, and later turned into an indulgence she'd afford herself. *"I don't know why you let the woman into the house."*

"I didn't. Keller did," Ryley said while rinsing the conditioner from her hair. She'd been expecting a minute alone in the bathroom. Time to recalibrate and relax. A minute to herself. There were no boundaries, not anymore.

"The nerve of that woman, coming into your house and telling you that you aren't being helpful. Can't she see that you've bent over backward and even hurt yourself trying to save her grandson?"

"I'm sure she doesn't see it that way," Ryley said. "How did the talk go with Tessa?"

"Exactly as I thought. She refuses to leave. She claims that her sister is now in more danger thanks to you."

For the love of all that was holy... "Tell her that I'll call Detective Crews before we go to Henley's house, and now, if you don't mind, I'd like to get out of the shower."

"So, who's stopping you? It's not like you have something I haven't seen before," Stretch retorted in bitter sarcasm.

"Stretch, this is the only time I have for myself. I need to figure out how I'm going to get Judge Henley off Tucker's back, and I can't think with you talking to me. Please, just give me a minute of peace."

"I'm sure you'll figure it out," Stretch said. *"I guess I'll*

go do some recon on that dreadful house from behind the gate; maybe I'll see something while no one is there."

"Good idea," Ryley said, reaching out of the shower and grabbing her towel. She wrapped it around herself and pulled the door open to find that she was finally alone in the confines of her bathroom. A reprieve she hoped lasted until she finished dressing, which it did.

Grabbing her bag, she checked her supplies again, this time adding the gun into her waistband and shoving the recorder into her arm sling. She was ready for anything, living or dead.

She opened her bedroom door. Tessa was pacing the hallway.

"Finally," Tessa said.

"Why are you in the hallway?" Ryley asked.

"Stretch said your room was off-limits. She said you were getting busy."

Ryley grinned. "Busy thinking. Nothing else."

"Oh. I thought..." Tessa said with a dismissive wave of her hand. *"Your cop friend is stirring up trouble. I was wrong to ask for help. I need him to stop before someone else gets hurt."*

That made Ryley pause on her way to the stairs. "Why the change of heart?"

Tessa frowned. *"I just need him to stop. Okay? I need it all to stop."*

"Tell me what's wrong. Tell me what happened." Ryley headed for the stairs and turned back when there was no answer. Tessa had vanished without a word.

Keller and Oscar were in the kitchen when she got downstairs. Oscar pulled out her chair and had her sit. He asked her to take off the arm sling, and he checked the bruising before tightening the strap almost painfully.

He pulled off her sock and poked and prodded at her foot. "The swelling is starting to recede on your foot, but it's going to be ugly."

"I've survived worse," Ryley said, playfully shoving him with her foot until he fell backward. "Now, leave my feet alone. They're sensitive."

"There is nothing sensitive about you." Oscar chuckled.

She rose and poured herself a cup of coffee and returned to the table to find Oscar putting a plate of bacon and eggs in front of her.

"Breakfast of champions," she teased.

"Well, seeing as this might be your last meal before fighting ghosts, it's the best I could do with what we had in the house."

"You must have been talking to Ada Mae, who clearly thinks I'm inadequate backup for her grandchild." Ryley grabbed the ketchup bottle and squeezed it as if squeezing the life out of the ghost that had started all of this.

"What did my grandmother say?" Keller paused with his fork to his mouth and lowered it without taking a bite.

"Just that I'm not good to you if I'm dead."

"Sorry. She can be a little dramatic," Keller offered.

"She also said she doesn't approve of the girl you are dating, but I say more power to you. Rock on and live your life."

He chuckled and smiled as if in approval. "You and I work well together."

"That's because I saved your life."

"By getting hurt," Oscar added.

She raised a challenging brow.

"What?" Oscar said with a shrug.

"If what Shelby said was true, then there is an entire house of killer ghosts waiting for us."

"Yeah, well, they don't know what I've got in store for them," Keller said.

His phone rang, and he answered. "Keller."

"Oh hi, Detective Crews. Thanks so much for

getting back to me." Keller shoved back from the table.

"Wait, I need to talk to him."

"Crews, Ryley needs to speak with you," Keller said before handing the phone over.

"Crews, what is going on with Tessa's case?"

"I'm still trying to locate the mechanic. He didn't show up for work," Crews said.

"And the Deadhead in the truck? Have you found him?"

"Ryley, I've had less than a day. I'm still trying to find the mechanic. The Deadhead guy is next on my list. I need to know what they were talking about in the video so I can catch the Deadhead bouncer driving the truck in a lie. Trust me on this. If I go in with the tape of him following her when leaving as my only ammunition, he can say it was pure coincidence."

"Well, I know it's not. How about forensics on the car?"

"It was ruled an accident, Ryley. The car is in our lot about to be returned to the family. I'm having a hard time convincing my superiors that this is murder. I'll need to reopen the case to justify the man-hours with forensics, and to reopen the case, I need some type of proof."

Ryley rubbed at her forming headache. "And we all know how much Sheriff Cavanaugh loves me."

"Exactly," Crews said. "I'm doing my best. Just tell Tessa to give me time. Oh, and the next time you talk to her, you might want to ask why she cashed out her college investment fund. Rumor has it she was using the money for drugs. Maybe she got in debt to these guys. See what other information you can find out on her end. I feel like we're flying blind."

Ryley wasn't about to tell him to drop the case as Tessa had demanded. There was something there. Something to be found. No one should be able to get away with murder.

No one but her. 'Cause when it came time to confront her criminal father, one of them wasn't walking away.

"She cashed out her college fund?"

"I went to the college to see if I could get her schedule, thinking maybe she crossed paths with people there. But I found out she dropped her classes six months ago. When I asked the parents about it, they were pissed. They had no idea."

"And her sister?"

"Her sister thought she was still going to class. She said when Tessa wasn't working at the pizza place, she was at school or babysitting."

"Wait. You said Tessa worked at the pizza place? Was it Ramone's?"

"Yeah, how did you know?"

"It's next to the mechanic's shop. But I'll ask her for more information."

"I'm doing my best, Ryley."

"I know you are. Thanks, Crews."

She handed the phone back to Keller, and Keller walked out of the room.

"I've got the morning off until the bar tonight. You have that look on your face."

"What look?" Ryley tried to stifle her grin.

"The one that says my leisurely morning has been canceled," Oscar said.

"I'm just confused. One minute Tessa is telling me she's been murdered and promises to haunt me until I warn her sister. So, I do, and then we find evidence that someone followed her from when she picked up her car. And now she wants us to drop the investigation."

"You didn't mention that to Crews."

Ryley shot him a look like...really?

"Okay, we aren't dropping it. Tell me what you want me to do."

"On the tape, there were some guys from the bar wearing Deadhead T-shirts. They went into the convenience store. Only one of the guys that got out of the same car was headed into the pizza place and wearing a uniform. I'm betting he's the connection for how all of these things tie together."

"Okay, so what do you want?"

"I guess I'm having pizza for lunch, and I know the perfect date."

"Keller looks like a cop; it's going to scare the guy," Oscar said.

"No, I don't."

"Yeah, you do," she said.

Pulling out her phone, she dialed the one person she thought might be able to pull this off.

Bane answered on the third ring. "No more news for you yet, princess."

Ryley grinned. "I need a lunch date."

"Aw, and here you thought of me. I'm growing on you, aren't I?"

"Get over yourself. Are you in?"

"I think I can fit you in my schedule."

"Perfect. We're having pizza at Ramone's between twelve-thirty and one."

"Noon, the cadaver dogs will be onsite," Keller said.

"Make that eleven."

"Was that the FBI guy?" Bane asked.

"Keller, and listen, I need you to not look like a cop. Can you handle that?"

"This sounds more like a job and less like a lunch date."

"It is. I'm going to need surveillance and background on one of the employees."

"What did they do? Piss you off by not giving you enough pepperoni?" Bane asked.

She chuckled. "No. I think they're connected to the murder of a ghost that doesn't want to cross."

"Oh, I know how much you love it when that happens," he teased. "Why not call Crews if it was a murder?"

"It was ruled an accident, and he's having a hard time getting the case reopened."

"Say no more."

"I'll see you at eleven."

"You've got it, princess." Bane hung up before she could reply.

"You're going to need your gun," Oscar said.

She pulled the gun from beneath her shirt and laid it on the table. "After the last few days, I'm ready for anything."

Ryley got the text from Logan just as she pulled into the parking lot. He was already there. She spotted his car and got out at the same time he did. He crossed the distance between them. His gaze assessed her arm and the limp in her gait.

"It looks like you've been pissing more people off. Who is it this time, living or dead?"

"Both." She grinned.

"Well, let's get you inside and off that foot. You can tell me who my target is and why the interest."

Logan pulled the door open for her, and she hobbled to the nearest booth and slid inside. The scent of Italian herbs and spices tickled her nose. Even after having had breakfast, she'd never turn down a slice of pizza. It wasn't in her DNA.

The waitress showed up and took their order before scurrying away.

"Who was it this time?"

Ryley heard the question but ignored it as she glanced around the pizza joint, hoping to spot the Deadhead who was working the day Tessa was killed.

"Ryley..." Logan touched her hand, turning her attention back to him. "You're making yourself conspicuous."

"Right. Sorry. I just wanted to make sure he's here."

"Who is he? Better yet, tell me who hurt you, and then you can tell me more about this case."

Logan Bane was a contradiction, much like Ryley. He'd been convicted of murder once before, only to have the conviction overturned. The police had tried to pin another murder on him, and he'd hired Tucker to get him off the hook. That was how she had met him. They'd been borderline friends ever since. He liked to walk the gray line as much as she did. That was why they got along.

So, she caught him up on everything going on with the case and how she'd managed to get hurt.

Logan sipped his iced tea as the pizza was placed

on the table. He waited for the waitress to leave before he spoke. "And why are we here?"

"Tessa. A dead college girl used to work here, and she was murdered."

"By a coworker?" Logan asked, taking a bite of his pizza.

Ryley shrugged and told him everything else she knew about Tessa's case.

"Is the Deadhead guy working?" Logan asked.

She frowned. "I haven't seen him yet."

"And you've got Crews working the case coming at it from a personal angle in search of evidence?"

"He's trying to locate the mechanic to question, and then going to interrogate the truck driver that followed Tessa out. He's looking for evidence, a lie, anything that will help him establish something else happened."

The door opened, and the pizza guy in question walked in. Ryley stared at him as he made his way past the tables toward the back.

"Petey, you're late," the waitress said in passing.

"I'm guessing that's our guy," Logan whispered.

Ryley nodded and picked at the cheese on top of her pizza; twirling it with a fork, she took a bite.

"That's just wrong on so many levels." He gestured to what she'd done.

"I had a big breakfast, but I can never turn down melted cheese. It's my weakness." She took another bite just to prove her point.

Logan made small talk, even as he covertly watched the counter behind them. "Looks like our guy is a delivery driver."

Ryley turned to find Pete shoving several pizza boxes into a heat-insulated container. He then headed back out the door.

"What did you say Tessa did here?"

"Tessa didn't say, and she's not talking to me now." Ryley sighed.

Logan downed his tea and winked at Ryley before getting up and heading for the counter. She turned and watched as he flirted with the waitress that had been waiting on them. She poured him a refill and batted her eyes several times.

He slipped her some money, and she quickly pocketed it before glancing over her shoulder and then writing something on her order pad before folding the paper and slipping it to him. A coy smile split her lips as she blushed when Logan walked back over to the table.

He slid back into the booth and shoved the slip into his pocket.

"One day, you're going to flirt with the wrong

girl, and it's going to come back to bite you on the butt."

"Today isn't that day." Logan grinned.

"Tessa only worked here for a month. She waited on tables and did the occasional deliveries if the drivers called in sick or were running late. She was bounced around from job to job while still in training. She was quiet, but Melody—"

"Who?"

Logan grinned. "Melody, our waitress, said that Tessa was quiet but that she kept a journal and was constantly taking notes about her job. Melody indicated that Tessa was kind of anal about wanting to get everything just right."

"You learned a lot in the couple of minutes you were talking to her."

"I told her that I owed Tessa a big tip, and I was here to give it to her. She offered everything else."

"I'm sure the money you slipped her helped."

"The tip had to go to someone." He grinned. "It never hurts to be generous. I got her number, too, if we need to keep playing that angle for more intel."

Ryley rolled her eyes. "Now I know why we pay you the big bucks."

"I'll tail the driver and see what else I can find out about Tessa and what she's hiding."

The door opened again, and this time Ryley knew the person walking in.

She pivoted her head and rested it in her hand, hiding her face from Tessa's sister.

"I'm guessing you know her or you're embarrassed to be seen with me."

"Tessa's sister, Ivy. I didn't know she worked here too, but last I saw her, I pissed her off. She's going to know you and I are here digging into Tessa's life."

He nodded and watched before leaning in. "She went into the back. You should head out, and I'll call you when I get something on the delivery kid."

"Perfect. Ooh, and Oscar's going to be calling you about another person to look for. A guy named Ethan."

"I'll reach out to Oscar when I leave."

"Thanks. I've actually got to go anyway and see a dog about a dead body." Ryley slipped some money out of her purse and left it on the table before getting out of the booth. She squeezed his shoulder in passing as she quickly hobbled out the door toward her car.

28

Ryley pulled in through the open gate at the Bateman property. A police cruiser was parked behind Keller's car. One of the deputies talked to a handler with a dog on a leash.

She got out and limped over.

"Right on time. You haven't missed anything yet. They just got here," Keller said as she approached.

"Great." She smiled at the deputy, who did nothing but frown back at her.

"Where do you want us to look first?" the dog handler asked.

"Out back," they both answered in unison.

"Where we know a dead body once lay," she whispered as the dog and handler moved to the back of the house. The cop walked behind them, sighing and grunting as if he was a bit put off by having been assigned to this case.

She ignored him as she followed. She stepped up on the back porch and out of the way.

"A reputable family used to live here. I'm not sure why you believe there are bones on the property," the cop said, leaning against the railing.

She remained quiet, trying to bite her tongue. She couldn't tell the cop what she'd been told. Not without divulging the cover-up of a crime.

The Batemans were a prominent family. She'd be ridiculed and branded a liar if she was wrong, if she relied a little too heavily on the witness and less on the evidence the sheriff was going to need. No way was this one being ruled an accident.

"What does he do when he finds something?" Ryley asked.

"He'll scratch at the spot then lay down and bark," Keller said as if he'd already asked the question.

The handler led the dog by the house, letting him sniff everything without lingering, before he started in a grid back and forth, stopping several times to sniff at trees. The morning sun beat down on the yard, making it look as innocent as the pizza delivery kid. Had she not witnessed Pete, the delivery driver, getting out of the Deadhead's car, she never would have associated the two.

The dog stopped and sniffed some more, clawing at the dirt before turning in circles. His tail and ears perked up.

Ryley slowly rose to stand. Was that the spot where Shelby's mother had laid?

"If a dead body was there a decade or longer ago, will the dog still be able to pick up on it?" She asked the handler.

"He can hit on a fraction of a bone a couple decades old."

"So even if a body was there and moved or buried somewhere else, then what does that mean for that spot?"

"Means there might still be a piece imbedded in the ground. We won't know until they dig." The handler planted a small orange flag to mark the spot.

The dog's nose went to the ground and started pulling the trainer away from the house.

"Looks like he's hitting on something," Ryley said.

"That looks promising," Keller said.

"Probably a dead bird for all we know," the cop said with a roll of his eyes.

Ryley and Keller were down the steps, headed in the direction of the handler through the unkempt acreage at the back of the house. She turned to look at the house before following Keller into the thicket.

A ghostly man was watching from the attic window. She slowly followed the others through the shrubs, carefully following the sound of the voices when she heard the dog bark.

She stepped into a little clearing to find the dog laying down in a spot that had little overgrowth. A spot right next to an old locked and forgotten storage shed.

"You have a key?" the handler asked.

Keller shook his head.

"I guess you'll need permission to cut the lock."

Keller made a call and got permission, handing his phone to the cop, who hemmed and hawed before handing it back.

"Let me go get my lock cutters," the cop grumbled as he walked away.

"I'll walk with you," Keller said, sounding aggravated that he was the one babysitting the cop and not the other way around.

"I like your dog. Can you train any dog to do that?" Ryley asked.

"It depends on if the dog in question has an aptitude for it. Ole John here used to work at the airport to spot drug smugglers and also with bomb squads.

He's retired from all that now, but he's still the sharpest tool in our tool shed. He'll get the job done."

"So, you think that he's found something?" Ryley asked.

"He lost the scent in the brush but picked up on something when he reached the shed. I'm not sure if it's the same scent, but I'd bet something is out there. He's hit on something deceased. Now what that something is, is yet to be determined."

Ryley peeked in through the dirt-caked windows, trying to get a better look. She couldn't see anything.

"You might want to step away from the window and not touch anything. If there is a dead body inside, you don't want to become a suspect."

Movement out of the corner of her eyes had her turning toward the trees in the distance. A shadowed figure floated just out of reach, watching them from afar.

Was that Ethan, or maybe his mother? Ryley would have called out for her if the dog trainer wasn't standing nearby. She would have gone and talked to her if she didn't have a witness.

The cadaver dog's growl was low in his throat, and Ryley turned to see the dog staring in the same direction she'd been watching.

Ryley frowned. "Does he do that often?"

"Sometimes if he perceives a threat."

She didn't ask what kind of threat. The ghost that had once been there just as quickly vanished.

Keller and the cop returned with the lock cutter. The cop snapped it and pulled the lock off.

Keller ushered him out of the way with a gun drawn as he entered the shed. The disgruntled cop flanked slowly behind.

"I told you there ain't nothing in there," the cop said as they reemerged.

"He's never wrong," the handler said, taking offense to the cop's comment.

He tugged John's collar and led the dog inside. He moved methodically through the structure, with all of them following until he came to a back wall. The dog pawed at it on his hind legs, turned on the spot, laid down, and barked.

"He's indicating the wall or whatever is behind it."

"Now, listen here. I wasn't authorized to be tearing down walls," the cop said.

Keller ignored him, pulled out some gloves, and shoved them over his fingers before picking up a nearby ax and hacking off the plywood wall.

He pulled it back, breaking the corner. "I'll be damned."

"What did you find?" Ryley asked as the cop peeked around Keller.

"That dog really can smell death," the cop grumbled as both he and Keller pulled out phones and started to call it in.

Ryley peeked behind the broken plywood to find a human skeleton.

"Good boy," Ryley said, and the handler gave her the treat to feed the dog. "Let's go find some more."

"More? You think there's more than one dead body on the premises?"

"Oh yeah. I'm guessing three or four. Let's go check the house."

Her day was getting better by the minute. With bones and lingering spirits, she really could move these ghosts along. Kicking and screaming, if need be. But gone nevertheless.

She stepped out to find Keller on his phone. She rested her hand on his arm, and he covered the phone.

"I need to touch one of those bones before it leaves the property."

A momentary confusion clouded his face before it cleared. "Your special thing?"

"I'll know what happened long before the

forensic team does, and not only that, my touch is guaranteed to move them along."

"I'll see what I can do," he answered.

She followed the dog handler back to the house while the cop was pacing next to his car. "Yes, sir. Yes, sir. Yes, sir. No, sir."

Whoever he was reporting to had the cop jittery, as if this was the first case where he'd worked a crime scene.

Ryley went into the house with the dog and the handler.

"Where do you want him to check next?"

"The basement and then the attic. Both give me the creeps. Let's start upstairs," she said, leading the way up the stairs. The dog sniffed in and out of just about every room as they made their way to the attic. The dog growled deep in his chest as he moved around the room, never hitting a single spot.

"It's creepy up here, but the only death is those animals." He gestured to the bird and rodent.

"I was sure those animal carcasses were practice for something much more nefarious."

He shrugged. "One would think. How about we finish checking the second floor by sniffing the rooms at the other end of the hallway, and then we can move back down to the first floor? That way, we cover the entire house."

Ryley gestured with a wave of her hand. "After you. He's free to roam anywhere."

The handler led the dog down the stairs, and Ryley was slower to follow. The heavy feeling of being watched settled against her shoulders.

They weren't alone. Someone was getting a bit antsy. The dog turned into the boy's room.

"What's the matter? Afraid you won't like what I find?" she whispered to whoever was watching nearby.

The dog moved fast through the boy's room. Sniffing here and there and even under the bed before casually trotting back out into the hall and into the next room.

Shelby's room was exactly how they'd left it. The dog sniffed the bathroom and the bed and into the closet. He nuzzled his nose between some new shoes, which looked as though they'd never been worn, and nudged them out of the way with his nose until he barked and laid down.

"This is the first closet for him," the handler announced.

Ryley flicked the light switch on and did her best to squat to get a closer look. The carpet looked no worse for wear. Some dust and age had taken hold, but nothing to indicate a dead body had been stashed in there.

A small discolored dot rested on the baseboard along with a single black feather. She sighed and shoved to stand, dialing Keller's number.

"Yeah."

"Hey, we had another hit in the little girl's closet. There is a speck of blood and a black feather," Ryley informed him.

"Perfect." Keller sighed. "I was hoping to keep it contained to the backyard. I guess not. Have the dog check the rest of the house. I have a forensic team coming in. We're going to be kicked out again while they work the areas."

"I can't be kicked out. I have a timeline to figure this mystery out."

"What are you talking about?" he asked.

It wasn't like she could tell him about the hearing and how her brother needed to have this done and over with. Would the judge give him a continuance if she didn't solve this puzzle in time? Or would he continue to let an innocent man rot in prison while a killer walked free?

The handler was waiting outside the door. "I'll give you the specifics later. We still have to check the master bedroom, the first floor, and the basement."

"Ryley, be careful."

"There are too many witnesses for anything to happen. These things like attacking when I'm alone or the opportunity presents itself, like on the balcony," Ryley said, hanging up.

She was going to need access to those bones more than ever if she was going to have any chance of getting things resolved before her brother went back to court that Monday. One weekend was all she had left, and now she'd be getting the boot by law enforcement. How was she ever going to win at this game?

The dog didn't hit anywhere else on the second floor, and they all went down the steps.

"It's clear on this level too. Where is the basement?"

She reluctantly pointed out the way. He opened the door and jogged down the steps.

The heaviness was back against her chest. Her heartbeat quickened with each step. A wave of nausea churned inside her body. Something dark was waiting downstairs. It was only a matter of whether the bones lived there too. An uneasiness settled in her gut.

The descent down the stairs turned cooler with each step. The dog and handler had already moved from the steps and had ventured somewhere out of sight. The walls were made of stone as if they were down in a cavern of sorts.

"Where did you go?" she called out to the dog handler. He reappeared in seconds, making her jump.

"This way," he called out, and she followed the sound of his voice through the dimly lit area.

The basement lights flickered above when she spotted the handler.

"It's even more creepy down here than it is in the attic," she said, rubbing at the goosebumps on her good arm.

"This is one of the oldest settlements in town."

"History buff?" she asked.

"It's always good to know where the bodies are buried in case John and I go for a walk."

Cadaver doggie humor, she surmised.

"Any hits?"

The dog took off, pulling away from the leash, and they were quick to follow. She followed the bouncing flashlight across the room to where the dog stopped. He stood on his hind legs again and scratched at the wall.

Then moved even farther down the same wall and did it several times before letting out more barks.

"This isn't good," the handler said.

"What, do we have a whole house full of bones?"

The handler rested his hand on the wall and swiped at the dirt that covered it. A name and date were carved into the stone.

"Yes."

"You're serious?" she asked, not expecting the point-blank answer.

"It looks like this house has its own tombs. Or it could be that the house was built over some type of burial site." He rested his hand on the stones. "These stones look like they might be from the original foundation."

"Are these Bateman family tombs? Why would anyone want to keep them in the house?"

"I'm not sure who these people are. They only have first names and a year." He moved down the wall, wiping off the dirt from the next six spots. A look of horror filled his face. "It looks like all the dates are within the last two decades. I think these tombs were added after the fact."

She rubbed at her forming headache. Six more

bodies and a drop of blood in the closet. No way would forensics get done with the house in time.

"Thanks." She petted John's head and scratched behind his ears. "I'll let Keller know what we found."

The trainer nodded, and they all headed back up the stairs, and she walked them out.

"I appreciate you coming out."

"Not a problem," the trainer said, putting the dog into his truck and giving him a treat. He pulled out a business card and handed it to her. "Let me know if there are any other areas you need to be searched."

"Thanks, I will." She waved as the truck pulled out, passing the incoming forensics van. The lead man in charge got out and came at her just as Keller appeared.

"Where are the bones?"

Keller pointed to the side of the house. "An abandoned building in the backyard. If you go around the side of the house, the deputy can show you where to go."

He nodded, and the forensic team headed off in that direction.

"How did it go in the house?" he asked.

Did she dare tell him the truth?

29

"Didn't you say your team is arriving today?" she asked.

He held her gaze as if reading her mind. "They'll be here tonight and investigating tomorrow. Why?"

"The dog hit like I told you."

"That's good. Forensics can get in and out of the closet before we start investigating tomorrow," Keller said.

She pulled him a little farther away and lowered her voice from any prying eyes or ears. "What if there's more?"

"Ryley? Did you find more?"

She ran her hand through her hair and frowned. "Listen, I don't have time for forensics to come in here. I have to clear the house of spirits, and I'm going to need access to those bones to do it."

"Ryley, what did you find?"

She frowned, debating whether to tell him the truth, knowing if she lied, she'd be liable for impeding a federal investigation. What kind of help to her brother could she be if she was locked up behind bars?

"It will be easier if I show you." She gestured to the house, and they went inside, shutting the door behind them and heading down the stairs.

The light above flickered when they hit bottom.

"It's over here." She gestured and used him as a crutch to help ease her throbbing foot. Her morning pain med had started to wane. She led him to the back wall and to the first tomb the dog had hit on. She gestured. "There were six hits."

He walked forward and rested his hand on the wall. "Only first names and a year."

"Yeah, and the years are recent, unlike an old family plot. The Batemans didn't have any extra family besides the husband and wife. There's no telling who these bodies belong to. It's not looking good for the Batemans," Ryley said.

"Well, we both knew the place was haunted. This is good news. It's proof."

"Not definitive," she said. "Listen, Henley only postponed my brother's case until Monday before he's going to rule on it."

"What does that have to do with this?" Keller asked.

"It's part of his blackmail. I can't prove it, but he said if I didn't get him answers and clean the house of spirits that he'd consider me a fraud and would need to question all of my brother's cases where I helped out and possibly throw them out."

Keller frowned with anger in his eyes. "That's how he got you to agree?"

"Yes, but it's his word against mine. He cut off the camera in the sheriff's department. He said no one would believe me, and he was right. Now, if you let forensics in the house and you show them all of this"—she gestured to the walls— "then I won't be able to deal with these ghosts, and if that happens, a wrong arrest can't be corrected and an innocent man will stay in jail, not to mention the real killer still walking free. My brother will lose his credibility, and I can only imagine what they'd do to me."

"Ryley, this is impeding a federal investigation."

"But, is it, though? You're here to investigate the threat to a federal judge. These dead bodies were here well before the judge bought the house. So technically, they aren't what you need to investigate."

"Ryley." His voice turned even more serious.

"Please. Just give me the weekend to figure out these ghosts and get them gone. Then you can come in here and dig up these crypts and burn the place down for all I care."

"Ryley..."

"Keller, these bodies have been down here for at least a decade. What are a few more days going to do in the grand scheme of things? I mean, really. And aren't your colleagues coming to investigate? I didn't keep it from you. You can make a 'federal' decision on how to proceed. Besides, you don't want your colleagues wasting an entire trip here. Answers are within reach; I can feel it."

Keller rubbed at his neck and let out a tired breath. "Fine, but forensics is going to cut out the carpet in the closet. I've already told them about that, and we don't know who the blood belongs to."

"Hopefully, it's just the bird."

"After the storage shed, they'll come inside, and I'll have them gone by morning.

She sighed. "I guess one day is better than nothing."

"I'll talk to Henley, or better yet, I'll have my boss

talk to the judge to explain that our hands are tied for the night. Maybe he'll give your brother an extension."

"Maybe, and maybe he'll grow a conscience and realize what he's doing is wrong." She knew as the words left her lips that he wouldn't do either.

"Can I get access to the bones in the shed?" Ryley asked.

"Not when they're here, but I'll talk to the ME about getting you access after he's done processing them for evidence."

Then it would be too late.

"Keller. In order for me to work my magic, I need the bones and the spirits on the same property. Across town isn't going to work."

"Fine, come on, but if this comes back to bite me in the ass, then I'm moving back here, and you'll never get rid of my grandmother or me."

The anticipation of getting answers excited her. They returned to the shed. Forensics had already torn out the wall entirely to see the skeletal remains out in the open.

"Everyone out," Keller said, flashing his badge.

The medical examiner rose from where he'd been squatting. "Keller. What's going on?"

"I need a minute with the bones."

The ME's lips thinned with irritation. "Don't contaminate my crime scene."

"We already have. We were the ones that found the bodies. Ryley pulled back the wall and reached inside. She's the one that touched and discovered the bones, so you're going to have to rule out her prints and DNA, along with mine."

The ME's nostrils flared, but if it bothered him, he didn't say. He accepted the answer without much fight.

The ME snapped his fingers and made a circle motion with his hands, pointing to the door. "You heard the man. Everyone out."

Finally, she was about to get some answers. She just hoped they were useful.

30

"Whatever you're going to do, make it fast," Keller said, walking back to the shed door and easing it closed from prying eyes.

She'd never had an audience before, much less another medium.

"What exactly are you going to do?"

"I feel the energy. It's one of my things. Normally, I can hold someone's hand under mine and put it on a casket, and if the spirit is around, the energetic zap can be felt through both hands. I've only done it once before."

"That's a neat trick."

"Yeah, well, since you're special, too, I'm kind of hoping that we could try it together with the actual bones and maybe you'll be able to see the same thing, too, and not just get your fingers zapped from touching a casket."

"What happens when you do it by yourself?" Keller asked.

"Touching a bone with a spirit nearby brings out an odd case of psychometry. I can see what brought on the death. Sometimes it's their last moments. Sometimes it's what led up to their death. It's never the same for each person, but it's always around the time of death. A moment in time that was important."

He nodded and took her hand. "Okay. Let's do this."

She gestured to the bone. "Your hand is going to be beneath mine. Are you okay with that?"

"I guess so," he said with a shake of the head.

She took his hand and rested it against the skull and put hers down on top of his. "Now, close your eyes and tell me if you feel the zap of the energy?"

Little tendrils of energy danced from the skull through his hand and up into her fingertips.

"That zap tells me that this spirit hasn't crossed."

He remained quiet, putting the rest of his palm down, as if wanting to experience the full effect.

"Okay, hold on tight," she whispered. "I don't know what to expect."

"Wha..."

Keller's words trailed off.

She and Keller were standing in the shed, only it wasn't old and dirty and run-down. It was still in the construction phase. The wall where the bones were hidden was only partially put on, and the rest were exposed beams.

"What the hell is this?" Keller asked.

"We're seeing a memory," she answered as the scene around them turned from day to night.

The door creaked open, and a teenage boy stepped in with a girl. He eased the door shut behind them. The boy was dressed like he was going to an expensive dinner. The girl was wearing jeans with a torn and stained shirt. She wore no makeup and was somewhat unkempt.

"Shelby, you shouldn't be here," the boy said. "If you get caught, they'll send you back, or worse. They know what you did. They found the bloody bird and the baseball bat in your closet."

Shelby shook her head. "They're killers, Ethan. These people aren't like us. They're ruthless. Did you see what they made me do to Mom?"

"You don't know that's who she was."

"Yes, I do. He told me who she was in the attic. He locked us in there with her. He said only one of us was leaving with him. He made me do it."

"You hit her with the bat," Ethan growled. "And then threw her out the window. You killed her."

"I hit her, but I didn't kill her. She jumped. She didn't want me to die."

He shook his head. "Why are you lying? I heard her scream. I was on the balcony. I saw her fall and you smiling. You pushed her."

"Ethan, I did it for us. I did it for you. Mr. Bateman said if I couldn't do it, then you were next. Ethan, that crazy man claims we're his children. That he had an affair with our mother and she gave us up without even telling him. You know why she did that?"

"No, you're lying."

"She gave us up because she knows what type of family this is. They're killers. She told me so, and look what he made me do in the attic. I didn't have a choice."

"Yes, you did. You killed her. That's why they sent you back."

Shelby shook her head. "No. You're wrong. They sent me back and told me that if I ever told anyone what happened, then they'd blame it on you. I had to leave, or they would have blamed the death on you. How do you think they've kept me silent all these years?"

"Stop lying!" Ethan yelled. "I'm going back to my birthday party. I've got to go."

Ethan turned to leave.

"Please, Ethan. Don't go. Not yet. I brought you a present."

Ethan glanced over his shoulder at his sister. "You killed our mom. I have nothing left to say to you."

Ethan turned to leave. Shelby grabbed a hammer and whacked Ethan on the back of the head.

He fell in an instant, as if dazed.

She bent over him, caging him in, and struck harder and faster until the life in Ethan's eyes blinked out and she was out of breath.

The surrounding scene vanished, and Keller's breath was heavy in her ears. "She lied to us."

"That's what she does," Ethan said as he appeared in the shed. *"She did this to me, and she kept the hammer as a souvenir, and I wasn't the last. Only now, she does it at work."* Ethan shimmered as though he was about to vanish.

"How do you know what she does for a living? Are you free to come and go off the property?" Ryley asked, thinking about the others that were blocked at the gate.

He shrugged. *"She comes back every year on my birthday. She has for twenty years."*

"How did she know about this place?" Ryley asked.

"She worked for the contractor off the books while she

was underage. She helped build this place. That's how she knew to put up the plywood."

He shimmered and turned to glance over his shoulder. *"The light is finally here."* A look of love so pure filled his eyes. *"Thank you for bringing the light back to this darkness. I couldn't have left without you."*

He vanished within seconds.

"Did that really just happen?" Keller asked, falling to his knees.

"Sorry, I should have warned you about the major energy drain," she said, gesturing to the door. "We have to hurry and get back up to the house. I have less than ten minutes, and then I'm going to be out like a light."

"A heads-up would have been nice," he said, stumbling to his feet. He pulled the door open and gestured to the ME. "It's all yours. You'll find my prints on the skull."

He nodded and swished past.

Keller helped Ryley through the woods. They'd made it just inside the door when she collapsed. He caught her just as the darkness sucked her under.

31

Ryley didn't need to open her eyes to know that she had somehow made it home. The familiar feel of her mattress had a calming effect on her soul, similar to what the heady smell of sage did for her nerves.

All was right in the world, except... Her eyes shot open.

The last time she'd been in her room, she'd had visitors of the ghostly kind. She hadn't had time to sage.

"You must be Ryley," a woman said, sitting in the chair across the room.

Ryley sat up a little slower, trying to reclaim her bearings. She was in her room. She was still wearing the same clothes. Only one thing she couldn't figure out. Who the hell was this woman? "Ghosts aren't allowed in my room."

"That's what I was told, and yet you didn't have any wards in place. No matter, I took care of that for you," the woman said, standing.

"Who the hell are you?" Ryley growled.

"My apologies. I was warned that you get kind of cranky when you wake up and you're hungry."

"I'm also cranky when strangers invade my room," Ryley said, and her gaze darted to the dresser across the room where her gun was sitting.

The woman's gaze followed Ryley's. "Oscar thought you'd feel safer with a weapon nearby, but there's no need for all that. I'm FBI Special Agent Jenna Spencer. So, we aren't strangers anymore."

"Who let you into my room?"

"Oscar and Agent Keller. They had to leave the house and asked me to stay with you."

"I don't need a babysitter," Ryley said, throwing her legs over the side of the bed.

"Oh, I'm no babysitter," Jenna said matter-of-factly. "I'm a witch. Well, I don't use that term in the bureau, but, well, I understand you and Keller can both see spirits, so I figure you'd understand."

"A witch?" Ryley said skeptically.

"What, you believe in psychics and can see spirits,

but you don't believe in spells and witches?" Jenna asked with a raised brow. "That's interesting coming from you." Jenna tilted her head as if confused. "Your magic is simmering beneath the surface, waiting to break free."

"Oh, I'm no witch."

"Uh-huh," Jenna said.

"Listen, you can be whoever or whatever you want to be. Don't let me tell you any different," Ryley said.

Jenna moved across the room and handed Ryley a drink. "Here, this should help."

Ryley drank it like she was dehydrated and just returning from the desert.

"My God. What was that?" Ryley asked, wiping her mouth with the back of her hand.

"An energy recipe that has been in my family for generations," Jenna answered.

Ryley's eyes widened. "That me that wasn't spelled."

Jenna grinned. "I could, but I'd be lying," Jenna said. "But now you won't pass out from energy drainage. I'll leave the recipe when we're done with the case. You can thank me later."

Ryley snapped her mouth closed. "You should tell a girl before you give her some type of voodoo potion."

"Oh, I'm a white witch. I don't deal with voodoo, but I know a guy, if that happens to be your thing."

"No," Ryley said, standing from the bed. "No, absolutely not my thing."

"Noted," Jenna said.

Ryley walked into the bathroom and shut the door behind her. "How long have I been out?"

"A day and a half," Jenna called out.

Ryley froze as she stared into the mirror. She shook out of her shocked state and threw open the bathroom door. "Where is my phone?"

"Downstairs in the kitchen," Jenna said.

Ryley ran for the door, with Jenna following behind her. "What's wrong?"

"What day is it?"

"Sunday afternoon. Now slow down and tell me what's wrong."

She didn't even know this lady, much less to tell her what was wrong. She ran into the kitchen and then paused, glancing down at her foot. The swelling was completely gone.

"How..."

"I'm a medical witch. The swelling in your foot was easy, just a family mixture, and I applied it like lotion. Your fractured arm is another story. It's going to take longer to heal."

"Thank you?" Ryley said, dialing her brother's number.

No answer.

Ryley dialed Keller.

No answer.

"Where the hell is everyone, and why aren't they answering their phones?"

"Amanda flatlined in her hospital room and was brought back. Keller was called to the hospital as her next of kin, and let's just say Judge Henley wasn't happy about that."

Okay, she could work with that. If Henley was preoccupied with worrying about Amanda, then surely, he wouldn't be at court in the morning.

"And where is Oscar?"

"The police called, and he said he had to go look for a friend. He said you'd understand."

Not hardly. None of this was making sense. Oscar wouldn't have ever left her alone with a stranger, and Keller, well, he might not have known better, but damn.

She grabbed her car keys and headed for the door.

"You're going to need this."

Ryley found the voice recorder device being held out to her. "Keller would be mad if you left this behind."

Ryley shrugged, but took it if it meant this woman would leave her alone.

"Where are you going?" Jenna asked.

"To see my brother," Ryley said.

"I'm afraid I can't let you do that," Jenna said, jumping in front of the door.

"Why not?" Ryley asked, debating how she was going to get this woman out of her way long enough to make it to her car.

"You won't win," Jenna said. "And I'm supposed to take you to the Bateman house. You have to give him proof, right?"

Proof that she didn't have time to find.

"You don't need to find it. We already did."

"We who?" Ryley asked.

"Our team. While you were sleeping, they found the proof you need for Henley."

"Great, so tell me what the name is, and I'll call him."

"It's not that simple."

"Sure, it is. Give me the name."

"Give me your keys."

"Why?"

Jenna nudged her hand a little harder in the air. "Give me your keys, and I'll drive while I explain. You shouldn't be behind the wheel. Not for twenty-four hours after drinking my mixture. Sometimes it has some bad effects."

Ryley frowned, debating on whether she was feeling any different from minutes ago. Her head was fogging a little, but not badly.

"Fine." Ryley handed her the keys. "I'm going to need that name."

"I'll tell you everything on the way."

Ryley's phone rang, and she answered as they headed out the door. "Yeah."

"Ryley, this is Crews."

"Oh, hey, Crews. Are you calling about Tessa?"

"Yeah. I'm going to need you to come to the station. I need to get a statement."

"A statement for what?"

"I need to verify that you were the reason Bane was on this case."

"Of course, I am. I asked Bane to tail the delivery driver and report back. Why?"

"Ryley, just come to the station. I found the Deadhead truck driver, and we have a problem."

"Is he dead?" Ryley asked.

"No. The driver is alive and kicking. He's not my concern."

"Then what is?"

"Bane is missing."

Fear slithered down Ryley's spine. Tessa had already lost her life, and now Bane had walked into the middle of her mess and was missing, too.

"Hang on," Ryley said, covering the receiver with the phone. "Detective Crews needs me to go to the police station."

"We'll stop there first," Jenna said.

"Okay, Crews, I'll be there in ten."

Ten minutes and Ryley would ditch this chick the first chance she got if it meant needing to find Bane. She'd just have to find another way to deal with Henley that didn't involve cops or the FBI.

32

Ryley texted Crews as she pulled into the parking lot. *I'm here. Meet me at the door.*

Ryley got out and hurried up the steps.

"Wait for me," Jenna called out. "You might need me."

Need her? Ryley ignored the comment and walked right into the building, where Crews had the security door propped, waiting for her.

"Thanks for coming." The door had started to shut when Jenna stopped it and flashed her badge.

Crews looked from her to Ryley. "New friend?"

"Keller's co-worker and my new babysitter."

"I'm not a babysitter," Jenna said, holding out her hand to Crews. "FBI Special Agent Jenna Spencer."

"Two FBI agents. That's a new record for you,"

Crews said, bypassing the interrogation room. He opened the conference room door and held it open.

Ryley stepped inside and ice filled her veins. The man sitting on the other side of the table was the Deadhead truck driver.

"What did you do to Bane?" Ryley lunged for him, only to have Crews hold her back.

"You know this guy?" Jenna asked. "Is he a threat to you, Ryley?"

"I wouldn't let anything happen to Ryley in here," Crews said as if disgusted.

"My job is to make sure no harm comes to Ryley St. James under any circumstances, and she seems to be agitated by this guy," Jenna said.

"I'm no threat to her. I don't even know her." The truck driver glared.

"Okay, everyone, just calm down," Crews said, gesturing to the chairs. "Have a seat."

Ryley sat on the edge of her seat, ready to jump at this guy's throat given the first opportunity.

"Ryley, Tessa's death was an accident," Crews said.

"You're lying," Ryley answered, turning her glare from Crews to the Deadhead truck driver. "You ran her off the road."

"No, I didn't," he said, sitting back comfortably, as

if death weren't imminent in his future. If this guy had anything to do with Bane's disappearance, his time left on Earth was limited.

"I saw you follow her. We have it on the security feed. You talked to the mechanic, and then you waited and followed her after she picked up her car. There is nothing you can do to change that fact. We have you on the security feed."

"Is that true?" Jenna asked, lacing her fingers together and sitting forward a little more, as if she were trying to feel this guy out, too.

"I did follow her," Deadhead truck driver announced. "I just wanted to talk to her before she ruined everything."

"What could she ruin?"

"That doesn't matter, but when she started driving erratically to get away from me, I slowed down to de-escalate the situation."

"How did your paint get on her bumper?"

Deadhead frowned. "My truck never touched her bumper."

Ryley turned to Crews.

"It's true. There's no paint on her bumper. I took pictures in case we couldn't get the investigation back open."

"Fine, but he still ran Tessa off the road," Ryley growled.

"She took the curve too fast and lost control."

"Because you were chasing her," Ryley growled, standing up.

Jenna put her hand on Ryley's arm. "If he's guilty, we'll find out."

"I'm not guilty of anything." The Deadhead truck driver rose to his feet, too. "I'm the one who called it in. I called an ambulance, but she was already gone when I got down the ravine. She was dead, and there was nothing I could do about it."

"I call that leaving the scene of an accident with a death. Isn't that a thing?" she asked, turning to Jenna.

"Yes. That's a thing." Jenna glared at Deadhead. "How do you explain that?"

"I couldn't be seen there and talking to cops. I would have blown my cover," the man said, retaking his seat.

Ryley retook hers, too. "What do you mean, cover?"

"Ryley, this is Officer Marcus Bay. He's DEA."

"No, he's not. He's a Deadhead. I saw him with the other guys."

Marcus pulled out his badge and tossed it to her.

She glanced at his picture and him and the badge in question.

"You did see me with the Deadheads. I was deep undercover. Their bar is run by a drug dealer."

"That still doesn't explain Tessa."

"I was undercover because I believed if I got close enough to the owners that I'd be led to the supplier. He was my target. The rest could be taken down after I got to the supplier."

"And?" Jenna asked as if she, too, was getting agitated that this guy wasn't getting to the point.

"I thought it all originated from the Deadhead bar. I was wrong. The supplier's contact isn't the bar owner. He's the bar owner's brother, Ramone. The bar owner was getting his supply delivered via the pizza boxes."

"The pizza place where Tessa works."

"Yeah, well. I had a confidential informant working at Ramone's. A college kid that I busted for drinking underage at a college party. He was already friends with some of the guys from Deadheads. It didn't take much to turn him into a confidential informant."

"The guy that works with Tessa."

"Pete and I had a system for passing information."

"The delivery driver?"

"Yes, and as you can imagine, we couldn't be seen together, but he could do his job."

"Delivering pizzas," she answered.

"Exactly. I'd call under a fake name once a week and order a pizza. He'd tape a note or a recording or whatever evidence he could to the inside of the pizza box. No one knew about our system. Then something went wrong."

"What?"

"I ordered the pizza, and Ms. Murphy showed up."

"Why did Tessa deliver when Pete was working? I thought she was just a floater for when someone called in sick."

"Pete got called to run a pizza to Deadheads at the same time. He had to pass off my pizza."

"She found the note?" Ryley asked.

"I'm not sure. The pizza that came didn't have a note. Didn't have anything. It was empty, and Pete swears he taped information inside the box."

"Someone got to the pizza before it was delivered?"

"Yeah, that's why I wanted to talk to her. I needed to know what happened to the contents."

"What did Pete say was in the pizza?"

"He overheard a meeting date and time. He wrote

it in code, something that no one would have figured out if they'd caught on about the pizza exchange."

"A meeting between who?" Ryley asked.

"Melody and the dealer. Ramone isn't the head guy in charge. His daughter Melody is."

"The waitress? Are you sure?"

"Yeah, I'm sure."

Ryley's heart stopped cold. "Oh no, no, no."

All eyes turned to her.

33

Ryley pulled out her phone and dialed Bane's number.

No answer.

"Ryley, what is it?"

"Bane flirted with Melody this morning. He was using her to gather information on Pete so we could figure out how he fit into all this."

"She probably suspects, and she could have done something to him," Crews said, jumping up.

"Do you have someone sitting on her apartment?" Jenna asked.

Talking resumed around Ryley, and yet she tuned it all out. Dialing the phone, she called Oscar. He answered on the first ring.

"Where are you, and why didn't you answer my call earlier?"

"I'm glad you're awake. I couldn't answer because I was with Keys."

Keys was the name Oscar used for his hacker. Someone Ryley still hadn't had the fortune of meeting.

"Tell me that your visit involved finding Bane."

"Yes. I knew you'd be upset if you let him walk into any harm, so while you were still out, I took it upon myself to follow up for you. Keys was kind enough to turn on the location finder on Bane's phone. I have his coordinates."

"Where is he?" she asked.

He rattled off an address that she didn't recognize.

"Who lives there?

"Melody Ramone."

"If you get there before me, don't engage. Just sit on the address," she said, disconnecting the call.

All the talking had stopped, and they were staring at her.

"Where is he?" Crews asked.

"Who were you talking to?" Jenna asked.

"Don't think for a minute I'm going to let you just blow my cover," Agent Bay announced.

"I need a ride. I got him into this. I can get him out."

"Just give us the address and we'll go in," Crews said.

"No," Ryley and Bay said at the same time. For once, they agreed.

"She's got too much to lose. Bullets will start flying, and then I'll have to shoot her. You don't want that, do you?" Ryley asked.

"Ryley." Crews crossed his arms over his chest.

He knew she would, even if all these new people didn't. Ryley wouldn't hesitate to kneecap someone who threatened harm to her family and friends. She'd already done it once for Crews. Bane wasn't any different.

"Come on, Ryley. I'll drive. I'm the only backup you need," Jenna said, heading for the door.

"Ryley. Let us handle this," Crews said in warning.

Ryley walked across the room and grabbed a piece of paper and wrote down the address.

"If you don't hear from me, come in with guns blazing. Or better yet, Oscar will be nearby, so come with a cleanup crew."

"You get into trouble, you call me. I don't care

who your new friends are," Crews said as if resigned to the fact that he couldn't control her.

"Rude," Jenna said in passing Crews. "But I'll allow it, this time."

Melody's house wasn't what Ryley expected. She'd expected a mansion or high-rise on the top floor with a few security guys. Something to suggest this woman was living lavishly on her drug money.

There was none of that. The condo was in a part of town that catered to older residents. She texted Oscar, who was sitting in his truck five feet away.

"Is this a mistake?"

"Nope. His phone is pinging at this location."

"Weird," Ryley said. "Okay, I'm going in."

She opened the door, and Jenna stopped her. "You've got ten minutes, and then I'm coming in to get you."

Ryley paused at that. "Why would you? And why does it matter if I get hurt? I mean, why are you acting like I'm so important to the FBI in the grand scheme of things? You know how to sage. You did it at my house. You could get rid of those ghosts."

She grinned. "Keller says you're important. I'm to

bring you to the Batemans' house in one piece, so that's what I'm going to do. If you have a problem with it, take it up with Keller."

"I just might," Ryley said, getting out of the car. She reopened the door and grabbed her bag. Unzipping it, she pulled out a gun and stashed it beneath her shirt.

"Well, now. Maybe Keller underestimates you," Jenna said with a smile.

Everyone always did. Ryley closed the door and limp-jogged across the street, surprised there still wasn't any pain in the move.

Taking a deep calming breath, she clicked the voice recorder on and knocked on the door.

Waiting a few seconds, for there to be no answer.

She rang the doorbell more than once.

No answer.

She kept ringing the bell and added some yelling to the mix.

"Logan, baby, you better not be in there cheating on me, or I swear you won't walk straight when I get done with you."

No answer.

She pounded on the door. "Logan, I'm serious. I promise I wasn't banging the pizza delivery driver. You have to believe me."

No answer.

"Please, baby. I'm trying to save our marriage. You don't want me to file divorce papers. Don't make me do it. You know I will."

No answer.

An elderly woman living next door peeked her head outside.

"Sorry," Ryley whispered.

"This is the most excitement I've had all day," the older lady said, grabbing the chair off her porch and moving into her grass for a better view of the show.

Ryley winked and started up again.

"Fine, I'll bring the cops back with me. You're breaking your house arrest. That's one way to keep you away from other women. I'll have you locked behind bars with only men. You want to go back to jail, baby? I swear I'll do it."

Melody yanked the door open and smoothed down her hair as if she'd been getting busy with Bane or possibly even torturing him.

"You must be at the wrong house, lady. There is no married man here." She glanced at the old woman in her chair. "Everything's fine, Gladys. You can go back inside."

"And miss all the fun? I don't think so," Gladys said.

"His SUV is parked right there." Ryley pointed to Bane's ride and then shoved her way inside. "Where is my husband?"

Ryley moved through the house.

"Logan, baby. Get your butt out here," Ryley called out.

Melody hurried to block Ryley's path into the hallway

"That's enough. I think you should leave."

"Logan, how could you cheat on me with our girls at home? You know they miss you. Come out and let's talk about this. I swear I wasn't screwing around with the pizza guy. I was just lonely," Ryley called out.

No answer.

"I know he's back there," Ryley said, laying it on thick. "I need to talk to him. He forgot to give me money for our baby's doctor appointment. I need to see him."

The door at the end of the hall opened, and Logan walked out, pulling his shirt over his head.

"Ryley, what are you doing here?"

Melody turned on him. "Are you married? Is this your wife?"

"No."

"How could you lie like that?" Ryley said, pushing

around Melody. She walked up to him, rested her hand on his chest, and winked.

"I'm sorry, sweetie." He finally got into the game. "I needed more than you were giving me."

"This is too much drama for me," Melody said, raising her hands in surrender. "Maybe you should take this outside."

Ryley wailed and rolled her eyes as she was doing it. "Get your things. We need to talk. My mom took the baby to her appointment, and I need you to come with me. They need both of our consent for the surgery."

"How did you know I was here?"

"Are you kidding? I saw you flirting with her at the pizza place. Please, baby, please come home." Ryley batted her eyes where Melody couldn't see.

"Wait. How did you find out where I lived?" Melody asked.

She was smarter than Ryley gave her credit for. Most women wouldn't be thinking straight with the all this drama.

"His phone is tied to my account. It was easy to track to the location and his car is parked right out front."

"I think you should leave," Melody said, crossing her arms over her chest. "Your daughter is at the doctor, and you're here sleeping with me."

Melody shook her head in disgust.

It would have been laughable if Ryley wasn't in character. The drug dealer had a moral conscience about married men.

"Fine." Logan went back into the room with Melody following him.

Ryley grabbed the cell phone on the table and slid it up into her sling.

Logan came out carrying his boots. "I'm sorry."

"Just go." Melody flung the door open, and Ryley walked out and over to Bane's car, pretending to argue until the door was slammed.

"What the hell was all that about? I was making progress."

"Yeah, well, I probably just saved your life again."

His brows dipped. "How do you mean?"

"She's the connection. She's a drug dealer."

"No, you're mistaken," Logan said, looking back at the condo.

"Am I?" Ryley asked, resting her hand on her hip. "The pizza delivery guy was a confidential informant for the DEA. You start asking questions about him, and Melody is going to get suspicious."

"That girl isn't some drug-dealing mastermind."

"Apparently, she is. Tessa stumbled into a DEA investigation, and it accidentally got her killed. Melody is running the whole show. Who better to sell drugs to college kids?"

"Someone that will blend in at parties and bars," he conceded.

"She has a whole network. She's the mastermind behind it all."

"Damn. I thought it was odd she kept offering me a drink. I bet she was going to spike it."

"Probably worse than that, once she got you under control."

Logan pulled her into a hug and kissed her forehead. It might look like they'd reconciled to any onlookers. "I see Oscar's truck. Is he the only backup you brought?"

"Crews and the DEA know where I am, and I came with Jenna."

"Who's Jenna?"

"An FBI agent that works with Keller."

He cupped her cheek and lowered his lips to hers, stopping right before. "I've got to make it look good."

"Actually, so do I," Ryley said, turning her cheek just as his lips came down.

She shoved at his chest and pointed to his car. Logan got in, and she leaned down as if to talk to him. She slipped the phone out of her sling. "I need you to deliver this to Crews and the DEA guy. I'm sure it will have the number of the supplier. I've got to get back to the Henley's haunted house."

"You came here for me?" Logan asked.

"Of course, I did."

He looked down at the phone. "Ryley, if she'd seen that you swiped her phone, she could have killed you."

"But she didn't. You might want to tell Crews to have his IT guys break into the locked phone and turn off the location setting when you get there. She'll eventually be looking for her phone, if she isn't already."

"Get out of here," he growled. "If she's as bad as you think she is, you need to leave."

"You first," she said.

Logan started the car and put it into Reverse, watching Ryley walk across the parking lot to where Jenna was waiting. She climbed in. "How did it go?"

Ryley clicked off the recorder. "Much better than I expected. The girl doesn't strike me as a drug lord mastermind."

"It takes all kinds."

"Are all your errands done?" Jenna asked. "I'm

afraid I have to insist we go to the Bateman house. They're waiting on us."

"What are they going to do during the middle of the day?"

"Ghosts don't sleep, dear. Just because you don't see them doesn't mean they're not around."

"You have a spell for that?" Ryley asked.

Jenna grinned and glanced in her direction. "As a matter of fact, I do. When you're ready to tap into your own magic, I'd be happy to show you how to use it."

"Exactly, how would that spell work?"

"I only use it on special occasions. It's like having flour rain down from the ceilings to show us where they're hiding."

34

Jenna pulled through the open gate, where Ada Mae, Tessa, and Stretch were waiting.

"Stop the car. I need a minute," Ryley said.

Jenna hit the brakes. "Can't you talk to them later? We kind of have work to do."

"You can see them too?" Ryley asked.

She gave her a look that said, Are you seriously asking me that question?

"Make it fast. For someone so worried about time, you sure don't seem to be in a hurry."

Jenna had a point. Time wasn't on Ryley's side.

She stepped outside the fence and watched as Jenna drove the car up the driveway and parked behind a succession of SUVs.

"*That woman,*" Stretch said, glaring at Jenna.

Ryley cocked a smile. "What's wrong with her?"

"She... she... she..." Stretch growled.

"*What your friend is trying to say is that there is something not quite right about that FBI agent,*" Ada Mae said, clutching the jewels at her neck.

"I don't know. I think she's been kind of helpful. She fixed my foot."

"*They don't like her because she won't listen to them,*" Tessa said, bored with the conversation.

"Why? Because she doesn't take orders?" Ryley asked.

"*No, like she really doesn't listen to them. She wears earbuds when they're around so that she doesn't have to talk to them.*"

"Ha!" Ryley blurted out and then covered her mouth with her hand. "Sorry. That's got to be annoying."

Ada Mae raised her eyebrow again. "*I told you that she wasn't right for my grandson.*"

Ryley's mouth parted, and she turned her gaze back up the drive to find Jenna tapping her watch and talking to another guy.

"She and Keller?" Ryley grinned. "I think they're perfect for each other."

"*Bite your tongue. She doesn't even own an evening gown, and have you seen her nails? She's in dire need of a manicure. The women in my family have to keep up appearances."*

"Ada Mae. She's a cop. Who better than to look out for Keller and watch his back?"

Ada Mae's brows pinched together, but she quit arguing.

Ryley turned to Tessa. "DEA knows about the drug dealer at the pizza place. The truck that followed you belonged to a DEA agent. He was trying to get you to stop so you didn't blow his cover."

She shook her head. *"No, why would he do that?"*

"He claims he slowed down when you started driving erratically. He said you lost control of the car and went into the ravine. He also said he called 911 for you, but you were already dead."

Tessa's frown deepened. *"DEA. Are you sure?"*

"I am. I looked at his badge. Your death was an accident. You weren't murdered, Tessa."

"I knew about the drugs. I got suspicious when Melody said she had forgotten something in the order. She caught me on the way out the door and took the pizza and returned a few minutes later. When I got back, I overheard her on the phone saying someone was on to the drug operation. They had to lie low. I thought it was the Deadhead guys."

"It's okay. The DEA agent is going to arrest them all. Your sister isn't in danger."

"Unless they think she's the snitch. That's why I cashed out my college fund. There's an attic opening in my closet at her house. The money is inside of it, along with my journal. It explains everything. I kept it close in case we needed to run. In case we needed a fresh start. It would have been enough to disappear and start over somewhere else."

"You should have told me everything."

"I didn't know he was DEA. I didn't know who to trust."

"You can go into the light now, Tessa. I'll take it from here. I'll make sure your sister and nephew are okay."

Hesitation cleared from her face. *"You promise?"*

"Absolutely," Ryley said. "As soon as I'm done here, I'll go over and tell her about the money and what's going on. I don't think Melody will be around much longer. DEA is probably going to pick her up now that I stole her phone."

"Maybe I should wait until you tell her. What if I leave and something happens?"

"Okay, but after I tell her, you promise to leave? I don't want to get a court order to dig up your bones and cross you over myself. That's no fun for anyone."

"*I promise,*" Tessa said. "*I'm going to my sister's, and I'll wait there.*" Tessa vanished.

"Stretch, do you mind?" Ryley raised her brow.

"*I am not a babysitter,*" Stretch said with a sigh.

"Please. I'll owe you."

Stretch grinned. "*Fine, and I'll hold you to that.*"

"I'm sure you will," Ryley said with a sigh.

Stretch vanished, too, leaving only Ada Mae behind.

"Don't you want to go to the hospital and check on Keller? I hear he and Amanda were getting chummy."

"*Bite your tongue. She's worse than the FBI agent. She doesn't even know how to shoot a gun, and her evening gowns leave little to the imagination.*"

Ryley grinned just as Ada Mae vanished too.

Ryley walked up the drive to find Jenna waiting. "That was impressive."

"I didn't even have to wear earbuds and pretend to be listening to music."

"How do you know I was pretending?" Jenna asked.

Ryley just grinned. She didn't know, but she

assumed. It was something Ryley had thought about doing more than once.

"Ready to go inside?"

Ryley headed for the stairs. "I'm ready for this to be over."

"Well, here's the thing. I planned to explain things in the car, but I didn't have the chance with all your drama."

"Okay, explain now."

Jenna hesitated. "Those ghosts. The ones inside. Well, they aren't your ordinary dead people, and they don't have any plans to vacate the premises anytime soon."

35

The living room with the dust-covered furniture had been transformed. Couches were pushed aside to make room for a table with monitors and computers sitting on top. Debris from the fire had been cleaned up. The energy in the house felt weirdly at odds, as if life and death were both trying to occupy the same space.

A man wearing headphones was watching the monitors, which gave him an eagle-eye view of the upstairs rooms. These people seemed to know what they were doing, trying to catch proof of the ghosts. She just hoped they knew how to get rid of them, too.

Jenna nudged the computer guy, and he yanked off his headset and stood.

"Ryley, this is Hedge."

"Is that really your first name?"

"Ron Hedge. I handle all the toys."

Ryley lifted her brows and nodded in understanding. Hedge was the equipment geek.

"He doesn't like to be called a geek," Jenna
whispered.

"Are you always in everyone's head?" Ryley asked.

"Unfortunately."

Couldn't you find a spell to stop that? Ryley thought,
curious to see if she'd get a reply.

"I've tried several. None have worked yet."

"Maybe you need to call that voodoo guy."

"You're so funny," Jenna deadpanned, as if that
would never be an option.

Another man walked in. His suit was pressed to
perfection. Now he looked like the man in charge of
dispatching the flying monkeys. The one that
everyone else would report to.

"Ryley St. James, this is special agent in charge,
Jack Hawkins, and you're right. He is in charge of all
the flying monkeys."

Ryley's lip twitched. She really should refine her
thinking while around Jenna, or this woman would
learn too many of her secrets.

"Yes, well..." The man held out his hand, and

Ryley paused, almost afraid to touch his hand. Almost like she knew if she did, something would never be the same.

"Sorry," Ryley said, holding up the sling to show him she couldn't really shake hands.

"Smart girl," Jenna whispered as she stepped around them. "Anyone heard from Keller?"

"He called in to see if you've arrived. He was worried you got sidetracked with Ryley."

"What? Was he afraid I was going to take her shopping or out to lunch?" Jenna asked, almost agitated.

"Well, you know there was that one time."

"It only happened once, and it was a necessity. The devilish clowns were scaring the amusement park workers. It couldn't be avoided." Jenna seemed almost pissed she had to keep explaining herself.

It was the only time Ryley had witnessed Jenna letting an emotion slip out since she'd met her.

"The last time it's going to happen, too," Jenna announced.

"As fun as the devilish clowns sound, let's get back to these ghosts. What is it going to take to evict them? A little holy water? Some spells? Whatever it is, I'm game." Ryley sighed and plopped down onto the sheet-covered couch.

"The evil that lives here isn't your typical ghost," computer boy, Hedge, announced.

"Okay, so what are we dealing with? And you better not say clowns."

"There are some normal ghosts here. Spirits of those that have passed but never crossed over, and then there is darker evil energy here. One that likes to play games. It takes on the form of whatever you want to see and then screws with you. For instance, if you're looking to connect with the previous owner, then that's who you'd see."

"But it would really be this...what? Evil thing?

"Shadow beings. A lot of death and despair happened on this land and in town. All that negative emotion has taken on a shape and had to go somewhere, and that would be what we're dealing with here."

"You've come across this before?"

"Yes," flying-monkey-wrangler suit-man answered. "Only this one is a bit different."

"In what way? Does it have two heads instead of one?"

"You should take this seriously," another woman said, walking into the room. She wasn't dressed like any FBI agent that Ryley had ever met.

Her flowered dress flowed to the ground and

shimmied as she moved. Her blond curled hair was styled in rivulets down her back. She looked like a transplant from the sixties.

"Ryley, this is Betina Grace. Bet, this is Ryley St. James."

"If you haven't noticed, your ghostly tagalongs can't get past the gate. There is a reason for that."

"And what might that be?"

"Someone long before us realized what was here and trapped it. My guess is that whoever did that couldn't get rid of it, either."

"How is this thing being kept here?"

"A trench was built around the property," the woman said. "Come with me, and I'll show you."

Ryley followed Betina out, along with all the others. What in the world had she gotten herself into? First it was a single FBI agent, and now they had multiplied.

Jenna walked beside Ryley. "She may look like she's from the '60s, but she's light-years ahead of all of us. She's the real deal. She's dealt with anything and everything you can imagine and lived to talk about it."

"Impressive."

"Yeah, just don't ask her about the scars on her legs."

Ryley's gaze dropped to the woman's dress. Her legs were covered entirely.

Betina grabbed a shovel from the porch in passing and headed straight for the fence. She dug to uncover where the pole went into the ground and pointed accusingly at it. "You see those markings?"

Ryley squatted but couldn't see anything. She went to brush off the dirt, but Jenna stopped her and shook her head. "You never touch another witch's work. Not without protection."

Witches. Again. Ryley sighed. Ghosts were one thing, and so were creepy crawlies. She'd learned to live with them, but witches, magic, and evil earth dwellers? Seriously? Didn't she have enough on her plate dealing with just the spirits?

If it aggravated Jenna, she didn't say. She pulled out a glove from her pocket and put it on, whispered a few words into the latex, and then brushed away the dirt, revealing something akin to what looked like runes.

"Whoever did this knew what they were doing. That is indeed a protection spell. Only it's backward. I can see how it would keep something in and create a barrier." Jenna sat back on her haunches.

"That black entity is evil. He gets inside people's heads. They'd feel sick. They'd do and say things out of character. I bet it could even compel someone to kill," Betina said. Years of wisdom shone behind her eyes.

"So, how do we get rid of it?" Ryley asked.

"We don't. That evil seeped out of the ground. It's grown stronger with time. It's here to stay," Betina said.

"And the only thing holding it in is this fence?" Ryley asked and gestured to the hole they'd created. "So, if someone were, to say, leave the gate open, the evil could escape?"

"No. There is some pipe that extends from one side of the driveway to the other. The barrier is beneath the earth and extends like a reinforced dome, which you can't see with the naked eye. That barrier is keeping this evil in."

Great. "But if the fence was torn down?"

"Let's be glad it wasn't," Betina said. "The whole town might become unhinged. As it is, the tunnels…"

"What tunnels?" Ryley asked.

"Never mind," Hawkins said, shrugging out of his suit coat. "Okay, so we're going to strengthen the stronghold until we find a way to get rid of it."

"If a barrier is in place, then how was it that I sent a spirit into the light? That should be impossible with this impregnable dome thing going on, right?"

They exchanged a confused look with each other.

"You crossed a spirit into the light on this property?" Betina asked.

"Well, yeah. It's a weird gift. I touch bones, and then the spirit has no choice but to transition."

"And you did that here, on this land?" Suit asked.

"From the shed in the backyard," she said, gesturing over her shoulder.

"And it's inside the fence?" Betina asked.

How many times was she going to have to spell it out for these people?

"Can you duplicate it?" Suit asked.

"Maybe? I'd need the spirit and the bones, and from the sounds of things, all the spirits that died here are still lingering." That explained so much. "Listen, I don't know how my ability works. It just does. It's not like it came with a manual."

"She would be useful in Memphis," Betina said.

"She really would," Jenna added.

"What's in Memphis?" Ryley asked.

"We can discuss it later," Hawkins said and walked back up the drive, with the group following him.

This was not good. Judge Henley wasn't going to

be happy one bit. Sitting on a property that couldn't in good conscience be sold, he was kind of stuck.

She still needed to give Judge Henley the name of whoever was haunting the place along with proof. The Ethan kid had died on the property, but he wasn't the only spirit or thing that resided within these property lines. It wasn't the house that should be feared; it was the land.

"What if we try to get the land blessed, or maybe we can try an exorcist? Would that work?" Ryley was grasping at straws. The desperation was loud in her voice.

"We've never encountered this," Betina said.

"It couldn't hurt to try," Jenna offered.

"Maybe if we started at one end of the property and worked in a grid to the other. We'd need an entire team of priests."

Well, hell. There went that idea. "Most of the clergy in town don't like me."

"I'm sure that's not true," Jenna said.

"It is. Trust me." Ryley sighed. They were out of options. Henley was going to ruin both Ryley and Tucker.

36

"Our investigation tonight should offer more clues."

She didn't need clues, if what they said was true. There was no getting out of her predicament.

"I need to run some errands."

"Again?" Jenna asked.

"Yeah. I have people depending on me."

"You can't just leave now," Betina said.

"There is nothing else I can do here. You said it yourself."

"We need to get a better grasp on the evil," Hedge said.

"I'm sure it will come out again tonight. I need to go. I have other obligations to take care of."

"Fine. I'll drive. You're still my charge until Keller releases me from duty."

Ryley sighed. "Fine. Take me to the hospital first, and I'll get you off the hook."

"Fair enough." Jenna grinned as she headed toward the door with a spring in her step.

"You'll be back tonight? You've already established a connection with this thing." Hedge asked.

"I'll be back. I just have other things that are a tad more important."

"More important than evil?" Betina asked as she walked back toward the house.

Ryley headed out the door without an answer for whatever the evil was plaguing the land and the house. Another couple of hours weren't going to change things.

Jenna was waiting at the door. "You'll have to forgive Bet. Her life revolves around her research. There are no vacations or time off in her vocabulary."

Jenna clicked the fob, and they both got into the car.

"I really do hope you come up with a plan to get rid of this thing. I'm not sure Henley is going to care if he sells it to some unsuspecting family." And if that were the case, then she'd really need to take the man down.

Ryley pointed the way to the hospital as she dialed her brother's number.

He answered on the second ring.

"Hey, Ryley. I was just going to call you to see how things are going."

"We found one set of bones, but it was for the adopted kid. There are more burials in the basement, but they only have first names and years."

"Well, crap. I was hoping this would be an easy one for you," Tucker said.

She sighed and lowered her head. "It's worse than that, Tuck. There's something on the property that can't be removed. Expect backlash."

"Ryley, you know I always cover my tracks. You may sometimes point me in the right direction, but I think we have enough proof for reasonable doubt in the Jennings case. If he rules against me, then I'll appeal until we get a judge that plays by the rules."

"I sure hope so. I'll call you later." Ryley said goodbye to her brother and hung up.

It wouldn't surprise her if the judge ruled against Tucker just to prove a point. He'd already blackmailed her into getting rid of the ghosts and finding the threat.

"Hmm." Jenna sighed in the seat next to her.

"Please get out of my head," Ryley said, resting her head against the seatback.

"Fine, I'll block you, but if what you were just thinking is true, then that doesn't bode well for you."

"Story of my life," Ryley said as Jenna pulled up to the hospital. She parked and didn't move to get out of the car.

"Are you coming in? I'm sure you'll want to hear Keller say it's okay to leave me alone." Ryley opened the door.

"Amanda is in there."

"And?" Ryley asked.

"I don't think I'm ready to see them together."

"Right." Ryley shut the door again, staying inside the car. "You know, when Keller first got here, he was in a hurry to get out of town. Something about him having a date."

Jenna looked in her direction but didn't speak.

"He was here to get divorce papers. I think it's fair to say that he's over her and he's moved on."

"You think?" Jenna asked.

"Yeah, I know. He's a good guy, Jenna. Don't let someone from the past ruin your future."

"Oh, well. I'm not even sure we have a future yet. We haven't been dating long."

"Yeah, I know. Ada Mae informed me."

"I'll never understand why that woman doesn't like me."

Ryley kept her thoughts to herself. "Let's go. The quicker you can get rid of me, the faster you can get back to the house to help flower lady and the suit man."

"Betina and Hawkins. You should really try to remember their names. You might need them one day," Jenna said, as if she could predict the future too.

"I know their names. I'm just screwing with you." Ryley chuckled.

"You're bad," Jenna said, following her out of the car. "You and I are going to be great friends."

Ryley didn't answer. She was learning to keep things out of her head while around this woman. "Okay, let's get this over with."

They headed into the hospital and stepped onto the elevator to go to the third floor. The elevator doors closed, and Jenna nudged Ryley's shoulder. "Thanks for the pep talk."

"Don't mention it. Oh, and if you want Ada Mae to see that you're the girl for Keller, just buy a dress and get your nails done. Once she sees you all dolled up and carrying a gun, I think her opinion might just change."

"This was all over a dress and no nail polish?" Jenna asked.

"Her words, not mine." Ryley shrugged. They stepped off the elevator and stopped at the nurses' station. She flashed her badge and got Amanda's room number.

As they rounded the corner, they found Judge Henley in the hallway, talking on his cell phone. When he spotted them, he held up his finger to still their words.

Jenna flashed her badge, and they both side-stepped him as if he wasn't important and entered the room.

Maybe Ryley and Jenna could be friends.

Keller was at the window looking down on the parking lot. Amanda was in bed with her eyes closed and an IV bag attached to her arm. The machine's constant beep suggested she was stable.

Amanda hadn't changed much since she'd dated Tucker. Maybe a few more wrinkles on her face and a new hairstyle.

"How is she?" Ryley asked, and Keller spun around. His gaze went first to her and then to Jenna.

When their eyes locked, Keller's entire demeanor

changed, and he relaxed. It was almost as if his soul recognized Jenna's as returning home from a long trip.

Ryley had never witnessed that kind of connection between two people. Matchmaker, she was not.

Ada Mae was wrong on so many levels. These two were meant to be together at a soul level.

Jenna's focus turned back to Ryley. "You say that's never happened?"

"Get out of my head," Ryley said. No way was she about to answer Jenna or try to explain to Keller what she'd just seen.

"What's never happened?" Keller asked.

"This isn't the time," Ryley said, gesturing to Amanda. "How is she doing?"

"She's been having complications staying stable. For the second time, they've put her in a medically induced coma."

"What do you mean she's having complications?"

"They brought her out of the coma the first time, and she was starting to respond. Then an hour later, before the detective even returned to get her statement of events, she flatlined while in her room. They can't explain what happened, so they're running more tests."

Ryley turned her attention to Amanda, clicking

the voice recorder on and off with her fingernail like a nervous tick. Hospitals made her anxious. The energy and death in the air seemed tenfold. The need to leave had Ryley's nervous habits out in full force. "At this rate, she might make you a widower before you're divorced."

"Rude." Jenna's tone was as sharp as broken glass.

"Sorry," Ryley said, taking Amanda's wrist and feeling for her pulse, ignoring the machines that suggested she was breathing fine.

This moment reminded her of her mother. Ryley had been too late to the hospital. Her mom was pronounced dead. Still, Ryley had checked her pulse to make sure it wasn't some type of cosmic mistake. The big difference was that her mom didn't have a pulse, unlike Amanda.

"What are you two doing here?" Keller asked.

"Tell Jenna that she's off duty. I need to go see Tessa's sister and talk to Crews about Shelby."

"I already spoke with the sheriff about Shelby. He's getting DNA to match the bones, and then he'll get a search warrant on her house to look for the hammer."

"They took your word for it? You didn't tell them about our trip down memory lane, did you?" Ryley asked with a raised brow.

"No." Keller chuckled. "Prints from the back of the plywood were proof enough to show she was a person of interest."

"Let's just hope that Ethan was correct and she kept the murder weapon."

Well, that was one case that would probably stand up in court.

"Did I miss something?" Jenna asked.

"Ryley showed me a neat trick. I'll have to explain more later," Keller said.

"Shelby is a nurse at this hospital. If we are to believe Ethan and what we saw, she's kind of unstable. I'm not sure I'd leave any friends within reach of that woman."

"I'm aware. It's why I haven't left yet."

"You're scared to leave Amanda alone?" Jenna asked.

"She's flatlined while alone in her room. Don't you find that a little suspicious?"

"We need to talk about this situation," Jenna said, taking a step in Keller's direction.

"On that note, I'm going to head out. I'll be back at the Bateman house tonight."

Jenna pressed her lips together. "You'll need your car keys."

Ryley shrugged. "You can drive it back to the

property. I'll catch a ride and pick it up tonight."

"Be careful, Ryley," Keller called out.

"I always am," she lied and clicked on the recorder while stepping out into the hallway.

"I know. I told you not to worry about it. I have it under control," Henley growled into the phone.

Under control wasn't the way Ryley would describe the look of anger on Henley's face. Ryley waited for the judge to notice her and hang up.

"Shouldn't you be at the house figuring out who the hell tried to kill Amanda?" The words spewed from Henley's lips.

Ryley swallowed around the lump in her throat. "I'm unable to cleanse the property you bought."

"I knew you were a fraud," he growled.

"It's not that. We did find bones yesterday, and I believe forensics is going to determine that they belong to a boy named Ethan. Someone the family had adopted."

"Are you saying there is more in the house than just him?"

"Sir, I'm saying that the house isn't the problem. The land is. There is no way to fix it."

"I warned you what would happen if you didn't fix my problem and give me proof about who or what pushed Amanda over the railing. I told you what was going to happen to your brother's current murder case and all the cases you might have been a part of. Are you still going to tell me that you can't fix this?"

"I can't fix evil." Henley, still living and breathing, was proof of that.

"Yeah, well, I can't fix your brother's case either. I'm going to have to side with the opposition and keep Jennings in jail while a murderer walks free. You left me no choice. You and your brother are as good as done in this town."

"Are you sure you want to do that, Judge? Do you realize how many laws you're violating with your blackmail and threats and now this?"

"I am the law, Ms. St. James. Grow up. It's your word against mine. Who are they going to believe? A little pissant woo-woo woman like yourself, or a respected judge who has a reputation for justice and fairness?"

Ryley raised her brow. "I guess they'll side with you." She frowned. "I'm doing one more walk-through tonight to see if I can help the spirits there to get out and away from the evil. Tomorrow it's all yours."

"I'll be sure to call Wilson's cousin and suggest that he take you back to court. I'm sure he'll be more than appreciative when I tell him that you're a fraud. He'll be one step closer to getting his hands on the Wilson Foundation money."

"I can't change the facts, Judge. Your property reeks of evil tidings. I'm not surprised you were attracted to it."

"Why, you little..." He lunged at her, only composing himself when a doctor walked by.

She wiggled her fingers. If he ruined Ryley and her brother was going down in a ball of flames, she was going to light some fires and take Henley down with them.

This town hadn't seen the kind of drama Ryley was capable of producing.

She stepped into the elevator and turned to find him still watching her. She clicked the recorder off and pulled it out of her sling, waving it at him as the door shut between them. Even if it wasn't usable evidence in court because he didn't know he was being recorded, it was still damning enough to cause a big, huge stink.

She may have recourse after all. How many years would she get in jail for blackmailing a judge if it were to backfire on her? Would it be worth it?

She only had a few hours left to ponder that answer before she'd have to decide once and for all.

37

Outside the hospital, Ryley called Crews, constantly looking over her shoulder while she waited for him to pick her up. Normally detectives had better things to do than to play chauffeur, and he'd told her so, until she'd explained where she was going.

Ivy Murphy, Tessa's sister, was skeptical the first time they'd met. She'd be even more so now if Ryley showed up without some type of authority figure.

They were going to have to explain the severity of the situation, and she was going to need to hear it from someone other than a crazy psychic fortunetelling lady. Even Henry, a man of the cloth, probably wouldn't suffice. No, she needed the badge this time, and Crews would have to do.

He picked her up in front of the hospital. "Bay

asked us to keep a lid on what's going on at the pizza place until they arrest Melody."

"I'm not surprised. Agent Bay is all about solving his case." Ryley glanced at him. "Did Logan give you the phone?"

"Yeah. Bay wasn't happy about how you obtained it, but now he has a better idea of everyone he's dealing with."

"He didn't even say thank you, did he?" Ryley asked.

Crews chuckled. "No. Not at all."

Ryley shrugged and turned back to the passing scenery. "Ivy doesn't believe in what I can do. That's why you're here."

"You finally need me?" Crews puffed out his chest like he'd won some unachievable prize.

"I just need her to hear me out, and I need to show her what Tessa left. You can confirm what I'm saying, and then we can leave and Tessa can finally rest in peace."

"How did she take the news that the Deadhead guy following her was DEA?"

"She was confused. I can't say I blame her, under the circumstances."

Crews parked in front of the white picket fence surrounding the bungalow. The grass was still in need of cutting but was clear of cluttered toys, unlike her neighbors'. A truck was parked on the street out front.

"Any idea who that is?" Crews asked.

She shook her head. "Not yet. How about we go find out?"

She got out of the SUV and walked through the gate. Ryley knocked on the door, and Crews was ready with the badge in hand.

The door swung open, only it wasn't Ivy's face that greeted them. It was her dad's.

His brows dipped as he glanced from Crews to Ryley. "What do you want?"

"I'm just here to talk to Ivy."

"We don't believe in your kind. Now leave us the hell alone," the man growled and stepped out as if advancing on Ryley.

Crews stopped him, flashing his badge between the man and Ryley. "Where's Ivy?"

The dad stepped back, even more confused. "You're a cop?"

"Detective Crews, and I'd like to speak with your daughter."

He wasn't quick to move.

"Now," Crews said.

"Dad, who's at the door?" Ivy asked, appearing

behind her dad with a burp cloth over her shoulder while patting the baby on the back.

"Ryley. What are you doing here?" Ivy asked, stepping around her dad.

"Can we talk?" Ryley asked.

"Now isn't a good time," Ivy said.

"You know this girl?" her dad accusingly asked.

"She's friends with Henry. She stopped by the other day to give her condolences," Ivy said, not telling her dad the entire truth. Ryley had stopped by, all right, but it was to warn Ivy that she might be in danger. "Can this wait?"

"No. I'm afraid it can't. You might be in danger."

"Not again." Ivy sighed.

"What do you mean again?" her dad demanded.

"Ryley said that Tessa wanted to warn me that I'm in danger. She said Tessa's accident was murder."

"Yeah, I was wrong about that. That's why I need to talk to you."

"She said she doesn't have time," her father said.

Tessa appeared next to her sister.

"Tes, Tes, Tes," the baby said, holding out his hands to the air behind him.

Ivy turned to look behind her with a frown.

"You have to warn her. You promised," Tessa said.

"Five minutes and this will be the last you see of me. I swear it," Ryley said.

"Now listen here, lady. I want you off this property," the dad said, grabbing Ryley by her injured arm.

Ryley looked down at the hand. "You're not very smart, are you?"

"Sir, remove your hand," Crews said, stepping up into the man's face.

"Dad, it's okay. Five minutes. What's the harm in hearing what she has to say?" Ivy stepped back, holding the door open farther.

Ryley stepped inside the house.

A baby bottle was on the table. A diaper bag was sitting on the couch.

"Excuse the mess. I was getting a bag ready for my mom and dad. They're helping with babysitting while I'm at work until I can find someone else."

Crews and the father followed her inside.

"Can we talk in private?" Ryley asked.

"Sure," she said, picking up the diaper bag and handing it to her dad. "Dad, why don't you go put the bag in your truck and grab the car seat. I'll be out in a minute."

The father hesitated.

"Come on. I'll give you a hand." Crews grabbed

the bag and shoved it against the guy's chest before picking up the car seat. Crews corralled the man and ushered him out the door.

"You're going to have to talk fast. My dad isn't going to leave us alone for long."

"There's no easy way to tell you this, but you can't go to work at the pizza place. Not today. Not again."

Ivy's mouth parted. "Of all the things I expected you to say, that wasn't one of them."

"It's a long story that you obviously don't have time for. Melody is dealing drugs from the pizza place, and the DEA is about to take her down. Your sister stumbled into the situation. She knew that place was bad news, so she cashed out her college fund so that the two of you could lie low and survive while staying off the radar while everything gets sorted out."

Ivy shook her head in disbelief. "Melody? She's like twenty years old. You're wrong."

"I'm not wrong. You're Tessa's unfinished business. She needed me to warn you."

"Okay." Ivy frowned. "You've warned me, but I have to get to work before I get fired."

"Have you not heard a word I said?"

"I have, but your words and warnings won't pay

the bills," Ivy said, narrowing her eyes.

"Right." Ryley headed for the hallway. "Where was your sister sleeping?"

"The first room on the right. Why?"

Ryley stepped into the room and stepped into the closet. Leaning against the wall was a step ladder. She unfolded it and climbed up it to the wedge leading to the attic crawl space. She pushed it open and reached around inside.

Finding a bag, she pulled it down and stepped off the ladder. Heading into the bedroom, she laid the bag on the bed and unzipped it.

"Tessa hid her money and her journal. She wanted you to have it, to keep you and her nephew safe and away from all the drama."

Ryley pulled out a journal and handed it to her.

Ivy laid the baby down on the bed and flipped through the pages. A picture fell out. She picked it up and dropped the book. The picture was of her father kissing a woman, only that woman wasn't their mother.

"Is that your dad?" Ryley asked.

Ivy flipped the picture over to discover a date on the back. A date from a month ago.

"This is around the time Tessa moved out." Ivy's words came out in a whisper. "Why didn't she tell me?" Ivy's voice rose an octave. "My poor mom."

Ryley took the picture and put it back into the book. She gestured to the bag of money. "You need to hide this until you're ready to deal with things. I'd suggest reading the entire journal before you decide to confront anyone."

Ivy grabbed the bag and re-zipped it, shoving everything back inside and under the bed.

"Tell her I'm sorry," Tessa said from the doorway.

"She's sorry you had to find out this way," Ryley said, gesturing to the empty space behind her.

"How did you know about the money and the journal?"

"Your sister," Ryley said. "I wasn't lying. You are her unfinished business. She cares about you. You were her rock."

A tear slid down Ivy's face. "She was mine."

"Ivy, let's go," her father called out from the living room, appearing in the doorway within seconds. He frowned. "What did you do to her?"

"She didn't do anything, Dad. I'm not feeling well. I think I'm going to call in sick and just stay home today."

"Sweetie, that isn't the responsible thing to do," the father said as if trying to talk sense into her.

"I'm sorry you came all this way. I'll take care of Justin today. I need him with me."

"What the hell did you say to her?" the dad growled.

Crews stepped in the way again. "Ryley, are you done?"

She nodded.

"Okay, let's go." Crews guided her to the door.

Ryley paused at the last minute. "You going to be okay?"

Ivy swiped at her tear and picked up the baby. "Yeah, I'll be fine.

"Not yet, but she will be," Tessa said.

Ryley nodded and followed Crews out the door.

"I'm glad you brought me along. That guy looked ready to rip your head off."

"Probably would have if you hadn't been with me."

He started the car but didn't pull out. "You want me to put a unit on her house until Melody is arrested?"

"Yeah. I do."

He grinned. "You know, I'm kind of a resourceful guy to have around, wouldn't you say?"

"Don't go pushing it." She grinned.

"Where to now?"

"Now I have to go to the Bateman house. Do you mind dropping me off?"

"Not a problem."

They weren't on the road ten minutes when she decided what needed to happen next. "Can I trust you, Crews?"

"I thought you'd figured that out by now," Crews said with a frown as if questioning why she even had to ask.

"I need a favor."

"Is it illegal?"

There was no easy way to answer that. "I need to stop by Logan Bane's office."

"So, it is illegal?" he asked.

There was no love lost between Crews and Bane. They'd both been cops, partners, at one time until Crews arrested Bane for murder, only to find out that he was wrong when someone else confessed. Neither one had really forgiven the other. Not yet.

She was like their go-between as their fences were starting to mend.

"Not really illegal. It's just a matter of whether I were to use the information."

"What information?" Crews asked.

"I sort of recorded Judge Henley."

"Ryley. Are you kidding me?" Crews gawked.

"Just listen. I'm not going to use it, but if something were to ever happen to me, he should be a suspect."

She rewound and clicked Play.

She started from the time they walked up to the judge.

"What was he talking about that he'd take care of?"

She shrugged. "I have no clue."

She started the recording again and let it play out through the entire threatening conversation between her and the judge.

"How would he even know that you have this if it was in your sling?"

"I sort of showed it to him as I got on the elevator. I wanted him to know that he wasn't as infallible as he thinks."

"You just had to have the upper hand. What is wrong with you?"

"Why do people always ask me that?" She shrugged. "I just think it's safe that I download this somewhere in the event that I also have an accident."

Crews tightened his grip on the wheel and did a U-turn in the street, heading back toward downtown and Logan's PI office.

"Blackmailing a federal judge will get you hard time."

"I haven't blackmailed anyone." Yet.

He glanced at her with a stubborn frown. "And you aren't going to, are you?"

She didn't answer. No need to lie to the detective.

"I just think it's best if I'm not the only one that has the recording if, say… Henley was to send someone to come after me one day."

"You're playing with fire."

"I wasn't the one to strike the match first. He was when he blackmailed me into getting the ghost off his property."

"Did you record that too?" he asked.

"No. I wasn't that smart. He turned off the cameras in the interrogation room the first time we met. I didn't realize the type of man I was dealing with, or I might have been better prepared."

"So, it's his word against yours, should your tape never see the light of day."

She turned to the window again. "Let's hope he doesn't call my bluff."

38

After a quick stop at Logan's office, where he downloaded the recording for safekeeping, Crews drove her out to the Bateman house. He let the SUV idle as they stared up at the building in question.

"I know you found bones so far, but is the place actually haunted?"

She slowly nodded. "No one should ever live on this property. It's rotten to the core."

"Good to know."

She opened the door and hopped out. Leaning in, she smiled. "Thanks for helping me today."

He grinned. "You're admitting you needed my help."

"I'm saying having you as a chauffeur didn't suck."

He chuckled as she shut the door and headed up the porch. She turned to watch him leave, worried the evil might try to keep him contained and ruin him too.

"He's smitten with you," Jenna said, appearing behind her.

"Now I know you didn't read that in his mind," Ryley said.

"Friends, then?" she asked as Jenna linked her arm through Ryley's and led her to the kitchen.

"I don't have friends," Ryley answered.

"That's sad," Jenna said, nudging her shoulder. "I already told you we're going to be great friends."

"You'll be gone in another twenty-four hours. I'm sure it won't take long for you to forget about me," Ryley said.

Jenna let go of her and poured them both a cup of coffee. "You underestimate your charisma."

Jenna sliced into a fresh apple pie from the diner and handed her a slice.

"How did you know?"

"Keller told me."

"Of course he did."

"I have a story to tell you, and I think you'll take it better if you're eating your favorite food."

That didn't sound ominous, not at all.

"After you left, it only took me fifteen minutes to finally put all the pieces together. We have options on how to handle this, but it's totally your choice."

"Why is it my choice?" Ryley used the plastic fork to dig into the pie. It didn't sound like she was going to like this story.

"Because I'm your friend and friends help friends. That's what friends do."

"Laying it on a little thick, but I'll bite, for now, friend. Okay. Fill me in on what happened and what my choices are, and I'll see if I agree."

"First, tell me what happened in the hallway when you left."

Ryley hesitated, debating if she should say whether she had a voice recording of Henley breaking about ten different laws.

Jenna grinned like she held all the secrets of the world. "That explains a lot."

"Damn it." Ryley really needed to learn how to block her thoughts. Maybe the voodoo witch could help.

"Well, I didn't know what you did when you left until now, but when Henley came back in the room, he had some major murderous thoughts in his head. First, I thought they were all about you."

"I have that effect on people." Ryley thought about the recording.

"But they weren't. He was calculating how long before Keller would leave so that he could try to kill Amanda again. He was debating how he was going to pay off his bookie with the life insurance money, and deciding what to use the rest on."

"Wait. I didn't think they were married yet."

"Oh, they aren't. Not yet, but after I left, I had Hedge look into things, and they each had a life insurance policy naming the other as the beneficiary."

"But I thought a ghost shoved her over the balcony," Ryley asked, confused.

"I'm not so sure about that," Hedge said, coming into the kitchen and cutting a piece of the pie. If Ryley had bought this pie, she would have stabbed Hedge's hand with her plastic knife. It might not have done much damage, but he would have gotten her point.

"Feisty and not a sharer," Jenna said. "I like it."

Hedge shook his head. "I think someone doctored the feed and tried to erase it, but didn't do a very good job. I'm still working on it, but knowing what we do now about Henley, I know I'm better than whoever he hired. I can find the proof that he had a hand in tossing her over the balcony."

Ryley swallowed hard and grabbed her coffee, taking a sip. "You mean you can prove this SOB is a killer?"

Her luck was changing.

"Hold your horses, missy," Jenna said. "Not only was he contemplating Amanda's untimely demise, but he was also working out a scenario where he could fit yours in, too."

"He's sending a hitman, isn't he?"

"Oh, no, dear. He doesn't want to waste money on you. Not with the debt he owes. He'll do it himself, and seeing how you are now the proud owner of a recording where he broke the law and incriminated himself, he'll probably want to make it hurt."

"Genius, by the way, not that you can use it in court," Hedge interrupted.

Jenna raised her brow.

"Continue. I know you've been waiting to get to the good stuff."

"What good stuff is there?" Ryley asked.

"He's coming for you. Tonight. I might have mentioned that the team has dinner reservations and that you'd be alone at the house by yourself. I was asking Keller if I thought you would be okay without anyone there."

"You're using me as bait." Ryley gawked. Damn. She should have thought of that plan.

"Yes. We figure if we leave you and Amanda alone for a couple of hours that he'll try one of you guys, probably you first, since the window of opportunity is small."

"Then again, the monetary reward is greater with Amanda. I've got odds he tries to do her in first," Hedge said.

"No, I think you're wrong. The hate in that man's head directed at Ryley was disgusting. I have every belief that he intends to do her in first and then bide his time with Amanda until things aren't so hot."

"Twenty bucks says Amanda."

"Fifty says Ryley," Jenna said.

"You're on," Hedge said, shaking her hand.

"Well, now that everyone is finished betting on my demise, I'm assuming you have a plan in place to catch this bastard red-handed."

"Actually, no. I haven't thought that far ahead," Jenna said, waiting a second and then smiling at something Hedge hadn't said aloud.

"Actually, I do. I set up cameras throughout the house, and I'll be monitoring out in the van. Keller will have eyes on Amanda's room, and I'll be watching movement in the house."

"So, I'll be here, unarmed, by myself?" Ryley asked.

"I think we both know that you're not unarmed," Jenna said with a raised brow.

Ryley grinned without comment. "So, you think if he comes after me that he'll do what? Incriminate himself, or you'll catch him for attempted murder?"

"I'm betting he does both." Jenna grinned. "So, are you in?"

"Just call me your bait, friend." Ryley grinned.

3 9

She broke down and warned Oscar about what was going to happen. He wasn't happy, but he offered his help.

She was debating on calling Logan next. No question; he'd have her back if she needed it. She repocketed her phone. No way was she going to get him involved in all this mess. If Henley survived, he would certainly throw his weight around to get Bane put back in jail.

The others came walking out on the porch, chatting about what they were going to be ordering from the restaurant.

"So, are you ready for this?" Jenna asked.

"As ready as I can be," she said.

"I started a fire for you, since there's a chill in the air," Hedge said.

Ryley's gaze shot to the house. "Oh no, no, no. We already had a mishap with the fireplace once before."

"Yeah, but last time you didn't have me monitoring things," Hedge said, patting her arm as if what he'd said was reassurance.

"If I die, I'm haunting you," she said with a raised brow.

"Actually, if you die, I doubt you'll be able to get off the property with the containment spell and all," Hedge said, winking as he passed.

Damn, she hadn't thought of that. If she died on the property, she'd be stuck there too.

She went back inside to watch from between the slats on the boarded windows, and for the first time in her life, she felt totally alone.

The crackling from the flickering fire was her only company. She stoked the fire, making sure it stayed contained.

Her vision was partially blocked, so she decided to move to the next level, hoping she'd have a better view of anyone advancing on the house in the front or the back.

For ten minutes, she went back and forth in her mind debating if she should just kill Henley or maim him. His word against hers kept replaying in her mind over and over again. Dead men couldn't talk.

Ten minutes after that, she was watching out the window again, at the empty driveway below, even as dusk started to settle in. She unbuckled her sling and stretched out her arm, unwilling to let her arm hinder her movement. A fractured clavicle wouldn't matter if she was dead. No way was she going into the afterlife wearing a sling.

If she were trying to kill someone, she'd wait even a little bit longer until she had the cover of night.

She stood just inside the master suite, looking at all the odds and ends that still remained on the old dresser, when a sinking filling settled in her stomach and the hairs on her neck stood on end.

She wasn't alone.

Slowly she turned in place.

"I heard you're stuck here," she called out, trying to rein in her feeling of dread.

The sound of movement in the hallway had her feet moving even before she'd settled on a destination.

She stopped in the hallway and closed her eyes, listening again.

Footsteps from above.

Her gaze shot to the ceiling, and she walked down the hall and threw open the attic door. Standing at the base of the steps, she flicked the light on above, forgetting the bulb was broken.

"You fooled me once. I'm not coming up there again. I have company coming and don't have time to get cornered in one place."

She shut the door and leaned against the wood, debating how long she was going to have to wait this out. What if Henley didn't come at her here? What if he waited until the next day or the day after that? One day was all it would take to ruin Tucker's court case.

She walked down the hallway and entered Ethan's room. The sorrow she had for the kid sat like a tight, heavy knot in her gut.

Ethan wasn't a killer, but his sister was. Had he been just surviving the entire time? Trying to fit in where he didn't belong?

No one would ever know.

Ryley hated her father, but couldn't imagine how her life would have turned out if Tucker had followed in their father's footsteps.

Rustling in the closet had her moving in that direction. She flicked on the light and pushed the clothes aside, looking for any ghosts that might be hiding inside.

Nothing.

She backed out of the closet, and the lightbulb above flickered. Then the light in the room and the hallway all went dark at once.

Her heart raced with each passing second. Would the security cameras even work without electricity? She turned on the flashlight in her phone and stepped out into the hallway, shining it in each direction.

She hurried to the stairs and jogged down them, still impressed by whatever voodoo that Jenna had done to her foot. She might just have to hire her out from under the FBI and keep her around for all of her medical needs. Not that Jenna would resign, not without Keller.

Ryley's phone light bobbed as she hit the ground floor. She moved to the cellar door, went down the stairs, and went in search of the electrical panel she'd seen only days before. Thankfully, it wasn't on the side with the tombs.

Without electricity, she'd be a sitting duck, and no way was she staying in the house, unable to see Henley coming at her. Nope, no light and this sting was over.

Shining her light in each direction, she crossed the room to the panel box, making sure that this wasn't some ploy to get her alone.

She yanked open the cover. Every one of the breakers had been tripped.

Her phone rang, and she glanced at the unknown number, ignoring it until she flicked the breakers back into place and was bathed in yellow light from above.

Ryley answered her cell. "Hello?"

"Hey, this is Hedge. Are you okay in there? The electricity went out as I was detecting some anomalies."

"I'm fine, just faulty breakers. Someone really needs to invest in a good electrician.

"Okay, well, now you have my number. Call me if something else comes up."

"Hey, Hedge..." Ryley paused. "Thanks for checking up on me."

"Keep your eyes open. Henley hasn't shown up at the hospital yet."

"I will." She disconnected the call.

One problem solved. Only a million more to go. As she headed for the stairs, her gaze fell on the tombs with the carved walls.

She strayed in that direction, taking a minute to

run her hand over the first name. Her fingers dug into the grooves. She'd get these people into the light and away from the evil. She had to. She couldn't in good conscience leave them here with the evil shadow thing.

Had that shadow evil thing killed these people, or had the family been truly responsible or influenced? She'd probably never know the truth.

She walked back up the stairs and had stepped out of the basement when she felt the hard barrel of a gun pressed into her side. The lights above flickered off again, thrusting the room into darkness once again.

"Have you come to see if I've gotten rid of the evil?" she asked.

He grabbed her by the bad arm. "You are the evil."

A gasp slipped free from her lips as he jostled her toward the stairs. Any hope of getting him on security feed was now long gone. His word against hers again, unless the cameras had caught him for a brief second while they were on. One brief second of him holding a gun would be all they needed to sway things her way.

Assuming she lived long enough to tell the tale.

40

If he only knew how messed up she really was, he might not be screwing with her or her family.

Her own gun lay heavy beneath her shirt.

He stumbled against the couch, painfully tightening his grip on her arm while using her as a crutch to prevent himself from falling.

"I'm guessing if you'd bothered to pay the light bill, you'd be able to see where you're going."

"I can see well enough," he said seconds before the butt of the barrel hit the side of her head.

She dropped to the ground as her vision darkened and blurred. Okay, maybe pissing the guy off wasn't one of her smartest moves, not by a long shot.

"Was that demonstration enough for you to realize I can still see, or do you need me to demonstrate it again?"

"Nope. You proved your point. Only now, when they find my body, they're going to know there was foul play. Explaining away the new bruise postmortem might be hard to do."

"Don't worry. I'll make it work." He grinned, holding her at gunpoint like the devil himself was lingering inside his mind and body. Had the judge spent too much time in this house, or was he always evil? "They didn't question the one on Amanda's face."

"So, it's true. You did try to kill her by throwing her over the ledge. Were you the one that doctored the security feed?"

"Yep. Kind of like what I'm going to do to yours." He grinned again. "You said it yourself. This place is haunted. I think you said that evil resides here. Sounds like the perfect patsy, don't you think?"

He yanked her to the stairs, pressing the barrel of the gun deeper into her side as he led her into the master suite and out onto the patio beyond.

"Going to do the same to me that you did to Amanda? Aren't you afraid I'll survive too?"

"I'm not worried about it. If the fall doesn't kill you, I brought along a little insurance this time." He pulled some seemingly empty syringes from his pocket. "A little air into the bloodstream ought to do the trick. Seeing how Amanda is going to get the same, I'm sure they'll find a way to blame it on the fall."

Dusk had settled into darkness. The group had been gone less than an hour. They were still at least an hour away.

"Aren't you afraid you're going to get caught?" she asked. "The others are due back any minute."

"Not with the service they're currently getting. My nephew is keeping them longer than normal."

"Wow, you've thought of everything. I'm kind of impressed," she said.

He motioned with his gun. "Over to the ledge."

She moved closer to the ledge without the railing she'd already dropped below. She kicked one of the small rock sized pieces of concrete left behind from when she'd knocked the railing off. The rock tumbled over the ledge, hitting the broken railing below. Soon her body might be just as broken.

"You kill me, what happens to my brother?" No way would she tell this bastard that she'd made a copy of the recording as a fail-safe. She'd never put her friends and family in danger.

"He'll start losing his cases. All the ones brought before me, of course. And I'll let it leak that you helped on some of his other ones. You'll have destroyed him from the grave."

"If I die, I won't be going into the light. I'll be staying to haunt you. Are you sure you want that?" she asked, steadying her feet.

The windy breeze brushed against her skin as perspiration cooled the sweat beading on her forehead. She held one hand out to the side to steady herself as if she were a surfer and the once glassy waves were turning turbulent beneath her feet. She slowly reached behind her back. If she was going down, she was taking him with her.

The hairs on her neck stood on end. She glanced down at the bushes below. All of the ghosts on the property stood watching and waiting, including the man from the attic before. There was no question she was about to join their ranks. Heaven help her. If she didn't survive this, she'd be stuck here too.

She would never be able to haunt the judge, especially if he didn't plan to return to the property. Would the light be bright enough to shine through the darkness in her soul after the life she'd lived?

Fear slithered down her spine, collecting in her stomach like acid.

Fire shot out the window below, sending the wood frame up in flames.

She gasped in shock and surprise.

"Perfect." He grinned. "A charred body will make it even harder to determine the cause of death."

Smoke billowed up from below.

"Looks like this is the only way down for both of us," she said. "How about you go first?"

"How about not." Henley raised the gun, and she turned as if to avoid it just as a shot rang out, sending her to floor of the balcony.

He walked over to her and kicked her ribs, sending her over the ledge.

She grunted in protest as she grappled for a hold. Her fingers barely caught the concrete ledge in time, struggling to hold herself up.

The gun that had been in her other hand fell to the ground below.

He grinned as he stared over the railing. "Looks like you missed your opportunity, but I won't miss mine."

Without Keller's help, there was no way she was going to survive this time.

Plumes of white smoke filtered out below. The

wooden boards on the windows below were fully engulfed as flames licked the dead vines, burning them to tinder. It was only a matter of time before the bushes caught, too.

She'd literally burn to death if she managed to remain where she was. This time, her only option was down. He pointed the gun in her direction and moved his foot to crush her fingers.

This was it for her.

"I'm not going to shoot you. I am going to watch you fall."

"Son of a…" His boot pressed heavier into her fingers, and she screamed into the night.

Images of her past traveled at lightspeed through her brain. The things she'd done. The things she hadn't. All the times that she'd wished Stretch would leave her alone and the plans they'd made in death. Now Ryley would be stuck on the property and only get to see Stretch from the other side of the fence. All their plans of haunting people would be ruined.

Sweat trickled into her eyes. Pain in the muscles of her arms screamed in agony.

The gun was beneath her. The maniac above her. The fire was about to claim her feet.

She had no choice. She found purchase with her feet, lifting them from the forming fire below.

With a single look, she shoved off with her feet and let go, flailing backward through the air. Hoping to hell she didn't land on the rusty railing.

41

Her arms and legs flailed on the way down as a scream burst free from her lips. She landed with a thud, knocking the air from her lungs.

She struggled to breathe. Her gun was just out of reach. She rolled to find Henley running the length of the balcony, looking for his own escape.

"Ryley!" Hedge yelled as he rounded the corner. He dropped to her side. "We've got to get you out of here. I called the fire department."

"Henley has a gun. He's still up there."

Hedge's gaze shot to the balcony where the judge ran into the girl's room, only to run back out, coughing from the smoke.

Hedge eased her up, almost afraid of where to touch her.

She clamped her arm to her side, fighting through the almost intolerable pain.

"Help!" the judge yelled at them. "She tried to kill me. You have to help get me down."

Hedge ignored him and drew Ryley's arm around his shoulder so she could use him as a crutch.

"The power went out. I knew I was done for," Ryley said, biting back the anger and tears as they swirled around like a pot of boiling stew about to bubble over.

"I thought it was the breaker again until I saw the flames."

She stopped him and bared her teeth through the pain as she retrieved her gun. She turned, keeping her weight on her good foot, and pointed the gun at Henley on the balcony above.

She inhaled several deep breaths to calm her racing heart. This man had to die.

Her finger moved to the trigger.

"Ryley, don't," Hedge said. "You kill him, and you go to jail."

"His word against mine, and the dead can't talk. Well, to anyone but me."

"I've got it on video."

She hesitated and lowered her gun only slightly.

"How did you get the video when the power was off?"

He gestured to the cameras in the trees. "I had a feeling he'd use the same tactic. All the cameras weren't in the house. The judge incriminated himself on the balcony. If he lives, he's going to jail. Now would you rather he die here on the property, or as someone's bitch behind bars?"

Her brow hitched. It wasn't a choice. Years of torment by the criminals he'd put behind bars or an eternity tied to the evil that had spawned on the property. "Here."

She lifted her gun again.

The windows burst out, and flames from the explosion sent debris flying from the second floor. Debris that included Henley.

He flew yards away. His suit was in a ball of flames.

She lowered the gun. Her breathing was heavy as Hedge eased her to the ground and went running for Henley to help put out the fire.

All she could do was watch as his screams died and his movements stilled. His charred remains were as black as the evil that now had him trapped.

His spirit lingered above his body, staring down at his remains. He was probably trying to process what had happened and how he came to be where he was.

He lifted his gaze to hers and narrowed his eyes. *"You did this."*

His spirit flashed in front of her, taking shape.

"No, Judge Henley, you did this."

"Where is my white light? Why am I still here?" he asked, turning in circles.

It might take an eternity for him to realize one wasn't coming for him. "You're stuck here with the evil you didn't believe in."

"But you moved the other spiri ont. You told me you did. You can do that for me, too."

"I could," Ryley said, turning toward the sound of the sirens headed in their direction. She turned her back on him and began limping around the building.

Hedge appeared at her side, wrapping her arm around his shoulder again. "He's dead."

"I know," Ryley said.

"Free me, damn it. Send me into the light as you did the other spirit."

The first fire truck pulled in, and men got out hollering and working the site. One came up to her. "Ambulance is on the way."

"I'll survive," she said, limping to the fence. "I'm just going to wait out there."

"The blaze killed a man. He's on the back lawn," Hedge announced.

Concern filled the fireman's eyes as he started barking louder orders and went running in that direction.

Henley's spirit followed them to the property line and to where the van was sitting out on the road. At the barrier, the judge was confused when he could no longer continue his haunt.

She grinned. "Enjoy eternity. I'm sure Amanda will sell me the land when I tell her how you tried to kill her more than once, and don't worry, Judge. I won't sell the land to anyone else. You and that evil eternity will need to learn to get along. Oh, and I guess now Amanda can cash in on *your* life insurance policy. She'll be all set."

"That's just mean," Hedge said, helping her limp away.

"No one ever said I was nice."

4 2

Hedge called the others en route to the hospital. She'd been swept into the emergency room again like a herded calf, only this time, they weren't so fast to let her go.

They insisted that she be admitted, pending more x-rays for broken bones and worry of internal bleeding.

Stretch had ridden with her in the ambulance. Not that Ryley could focus enough to talk to her. The ER had been the same story. Question after question about past history, with the worry of what might have actually happened. Worry and prodding as if a significant other might have thrown her over the balcony. No one believed her when she told them Judge Henley had done the honors.

Oscar and her brother were quick to arrive, questioning the doctors and nurses like they were the ones holding medical degrees. Ryley could only watch on in silent amusement.

The door opened again, and she expected another doctor demanding tests and was met with Keller's stern face.

Oscar moved to her side as if Keller were the bad guy in all this.

"You were supposed to protect her. Where were you?" her brother demanded.

"He was guarding Amanda. Henley had tried to kill her twice, and she was in a coma. She couldn't protect herself."

"Yeah, well, he protected her just fine, you not so much. You should have had more backup!" Oscar exclaimed.

"I'm alive," Ryley said.

"A little worse for wear," Tucker added.

"Can I have a minute?" Keller asked.

"Sure," Ryley said.

Oscar and Tucker didn't make a move to leave.

"Alone," Keller added.

"Go. I need a break from you guys, anyway. You're hovering worse than my mother," Ryley said, shooing them out the door.

Oscar squeezed her hand. "I'm not going far. I'll just be outside the door."

"I'm not going far either," Tucker added.

"Could one of you extend your wait and go as far as the cafeteria and bring me back some coffee?"

Keller's lip twitched.

Oscar and Tucker headed for the door. "Oh, and sneak me in some chocolate, too. I love you guys."

Tucker waved his hand as he left.

Keller waited for the door to shut before he took up the vacated position by Ryley's bed.

"You look like hell."

"An evil judge and tainted land will do that to a girl," Ryley said.

"I'm sorry I wasn't there. If I'd known they were going to use you for bait and leave only Hedge as the lookout, I never would have agreed to their plan."

"It worked," she said with a shrug and then cringed at the arm movement.

Keller frowned at her cringe.

"How's Amanda?" Ryley asked.

"She woke up from her coma. She confirmed what Jenna had already found out, reading the judge's mind. Amanda confirmed their suspicion. The judge had been in her room, messing with her IV bags before she coded each time. He was also the one that pushed her off the balcony. She thinks he would have left her there to die if a neighbor hadn't called the police."

"She got lucky. I'm glad she's okay. I'm going to need her to get better."

"Why is that?"

"I need her to sell me that property," Ryley said with a grin.

Keller's brows pulled together.

"The judge is stuck there with the evil." Ryley grinned triumphantly. "That land will never be sold again."

Keller's confused look gave way to a grin. "I'll let her know you want it. I'm sure she'll be glad to get it off her hands."

The door opened again, and Jenna walked in with Jack Hawkins.

"Have you asked her?" Jenna said, coming to the other side of the bed.

"Asked me what?" Ryley asked.

"I guess not," Jenna said. "I was sure we gave you enough time."

"You did. I just think that I already know her answer," Keller said. "I don't even need to be a mind reader."

"Ask me what?" Ryley repeated.

Hawkins stood at the end of the bed and crossed his arms over his chest.

"Give me a few minutes with Ms. St. James."

The other two hesitated until Hawkins gave Keller the stare. It probably worked on a lot of people in his line of work.

It wouldn't have worked on her.

Jenna and Keller reluctantly stepped out of the room. Hawkins waited for the door to shut.

"You're a pain in the ass, Ms. St. James," he announced.

"I try, Jack. Can I call you Jack? Or would you prefer flying-monkey wrangler?" Ryley said, adjusting on the bed in search of a comfortable position.

"Jack is fine for now," he said. "My entire team is special, just like you."

"Is this your awkward way of trying to recruit me?" she asked. "'Cause I've got to tell you. I'd never pass your background check."

Jack's facial features didn't give away what he was thinking. He was a hard man to read.

"I know all about your background, Ms. St. James."

"If that's so, then you know I hate to be called by my last name."

"Ryley," he conceded. "You've done the govern-ment a huge favor, bringing to light the illegal actions of a federal judge."

"Are you going to give me a medal?"

"Our work flies under the radar, so no medal, not this time, but we do have room on our team for you if you're interested in helping us on our quest."

"I don't have to research the paranormal to know that they exist. I can see them, and they take great pleasure in annoying me. I think I have enough ghosts to contend with for now."

"We aren't typical FBI, and we aren't ghost hunters. We're somewhere in between. We excel in cases where common answers aren't always found and where evil still survives in the afterlife, where spirits manipulate the living."

"Fun as that sounds, I think I'll pass."

"We could use you. You seem to have a talent for pissing spirits off."

"You want to hire me as bait?" Ryley chuckled.

"Well, that and Jenna seems to have taken a shine to you. And she doesn't like just anyone. She's in need of a partner."

"I think Keller is more her speed," Ryley said.

Jack's facial features hardened, as if just hearing

that suggestion was wrong. The first emotional response.

"I'm not so sure about that."

Ryley shrugged and then regretted it again. "My family is here. I have a life here. I have two businesses to run. I'm afraid I don't have much time for outside sports."

Jack grinned, and his shoulders seemed to relax a little.

"It is a sport for you, isn't it?"

"I help where I can, although I don't think I'll ever win at this game."

He dropped his defensive pose and slid his hands into his pockets. "Maybe you should try keeping score. It might make things more interesting."

Ryley smiled, the first genuine smile she'd felt in a long time. "I'll do that."

He headed for the door. "I'll let you get some rest."

As he pulled the door open, Ryley called out. "If you ever have a case that you just can't solve, you can call. If you've got an opening in your lineup, I'll join your team as a pinch hitter, but only on special occasions that warrant it."

"I'll keep that in mind," he said, taking out a card from his wallet. He walked back across the room and put the card on the table next to her. "And when you need me, or you get into a game that's over your head, feel free to reach out. We're all on the same team."

He headed for the door.

"Hey, Jack!" she called out.

He turned with a raised brow. "Yeah."

"Can you make speeding tickets disappear?"

He grinned. "Yeah, I can for the people on my team."

Team was an unfamiliar word to Ryley. She might not have a group of people with special abilities like hers, or even better ones, but she was building her own team of sorts. Friends that helped her in a jam, a family that would never walk away, and an assistant who was worth more than any diamonds she'd ever stolen.

Her place was in this town with them. Helping them and watching their backs as only she could do.

He pulled the door open. "Our next stop is Memphis, if you change your mind."

"Hey, what's in Memphis? You never told me," she called out.

Jack grinned as he walked out the door.

CHAPTER 43

"Ryley, what are you doing?" Stretch asked from the doorway where a fresh new line of salt had been added.

"I'm just putting some stuff up," Ryley said, unfolding the step ladder and stepping up on it.

"I can't get in," Stretch said, sounding upset.

"Neither can any of the others," Ryley called out, pulling down a box from the top shelf. She stepped off the ladder, lowered the box to the floor, and opened it.

"I understand the others, but why won't you let me in?"

"I'm not a witch with a fancy spell."

"You could be," she called out. "It runs in your

family along with a lot of other things, if you ever just decide to embrace your roots."

Ryley didn't even want to know what that meant. She pulled out the spelled gloves that Jenna had given her. She snapped them carefully onto her hands.

Unzipping the FBI backpack Keller had given her as a thank-you gift, she pulled out the red satin scarf with ancient spells drawn on the material in black marker.

A small bone rested in the spelled satin bed. A way to change her mind if she ever grew a conscience. One of Henley's bones, should she ever decide to forgive him and want to move him on. Decisions had been made for her through her whole life. This decision was solely hers. She held all the cards now.

"Oscar just pulled into the drive," Stretch said.

Ryley placed the bone back in the backpack and then shoved it inside the box. She pushed the box next to her shoes, unable to lift it up onto her top shelf until her arm was better.

She stepped out of the closet and shut the door just as Oscar appeared at her bedroom doorway. He was quick to recognize the salt line, and stilled.

"Is that for me, too?"

"Everyone," she said.

"We need to leave, or we're going to be late."

"Late is such a relative word. Henley's spirit wasn't going anywhere for all of eternity," she said, following Oscar out of the room.

This drive across town to the Bateman house was much more relaxed than all the other times she'd gone.

"I got a call from Crews. They arrested Melody."

"That's outstanding."

"And the Wilson Foundation has followed through, picking Ivy Murphy as the latest recipient. She now has a solid home with heightened security that is paid for, free and clear."

"I bet Tessa would have loved that." Ryley grinned. Helping people in her own special way felt right.

"Drug runners off the street, a single mom now has much better financial footing, and you managed to stay alive. You did well," Oscar said.

She had barely gotten herself out of this jam.

"I'm looking forward to getting life back to normal after Memphis," she said.

"So, you decided to help the FBI team out again? I thought you were done working with them."

She shrugged. "I'm in need of a vacation."

"So is Kent. We need to work on finding you some help."

Her overworked bartender was something she'd need to deal with sooner rather than later. She had even more time-consuming, pressing problems on her plate she hadn't dealt with, including dealing with the mortuary beautician assistant Pete Roth's evil cloud. That was coming whether she liked it or not.

Her screwed-up world was most certainly back to normal.

They pulled in to find the construction crew on-site.

The construction foreman approached and handed them both hard hats.

Henley glared in her direction. An evil dark shadow lingered just inside the tree line, filling her veins with unwarranted dread. There would be a time she'd need to deal with whatever the heck that was, but for now it was contained. She just hoped it stayed that way.

There hadn't been much left of the six crypts in the basement, but there was enough for Ryley to touch pieces of bones and send those spirits along. When doing so, she'd seen just how depraved the Batemans had been, hiring only new staff that didn't have anyone who would miss them and then killing them for sport.

They rested in peace now, unlike Henley.

"Tell him to go ahead," she said to the foreman, who gave a signal to the man in the machine.

The wrecking ball rose and flew through the air with a silent swing, sending the charred remains of the creepy house down to the ground.

"Make sure they tear down just the house. That fence isn't so much as to be breathed on." She might even call Jenna to see if she and her witchy friends could come back and strengthen the wards already in place.

"You're the boss."

Yes, she was.

With the demolition underway, they headed back to Oscar's truck. He got in.

"Ryley!" Henley called out.

"I've nothing to say to you."

"I've got a proposition for you."

She slowed and turned in place. "What could you possibly have to offer that I need?"

"I know things about the people in this town. I've seen things. I could help you."

The offer lingered in her mind as she stared at

him. If she went down this road, she'd be no better than him.

She walked back to the gate again.

"What did you have in mind?"

If you enjoyed book 2, Grave Mistake, please consider leaving a review.

If you want more Ryley shenanigans, then check out Grave Shelter, book 3 on Amazon where the ghosts are hard to control, just like the new guy in Ryley's life.

Want to try another series? How about Fractured Minds?
All of my books are in Kindle Unlimited.

Want more? Sign up for my newsletter to get notified for future releases. All Books. No spam.

ABOUT THE AUTHOR

Kate Allenton loves reading and writing everything, romance, mystery, and suspense while including a supernatural flare.

She offers a reading escape where strong women with special abilities have to fight for their happily-ever-after and sometimes the line between good and evil is blurred.

Most of her books are set in Florida because she craves sunlight. If she had to choose between being psychic or having a super power, she'd pick psychic every time.

She was a 2014 Rom Con Reader Finalist in Romantic Suspense for her book, Deadly Desire (Carrington-Hill Investigations). In 2017 her book, Maid of Honor, in the Wedding Dreams Box Set hit the USA Today Bestsellers List.

Sign up for her newsletters HERE

She loves to hear from her readers by email at
KateAllenton@hotmail.com, on
Twitter@KateAllenton, and on Facebook at
facebook.com/kateallenton.1
Visit her website at www.kateallenton.com

Dead Famous (Book 3)

Deadly Ties (Book 4)

Deadly Bliss (Book 5)

Deadly Flirtations (Book 6)

THE HEX SISTER MYSTERIES

Witch Unleashed (Book 1)

Witchy Trouble (Book 2)

Witch Bait (Book 3)

Witchy Warning (Book 4)

Witchy Past (Book 5)

Witch Hunt (Book 6)

BENNETT SISTERS

Intuition (Book 1)

Touch of Fate (Book 2)

Mind Play (Book 3)

The Reckoning (Book 4)

Redemption (Book 5)

Chance Encounters (Book 6)

Destined Hearts (Book 7)

BENNETT DYNASTY

Rotten Apple (Book 1)

Pay Dirt (Book2)

Down & Dirty (Book 3)

Hard To Hold (Book 4)

Sour Layer (Book 5)

Train Wreck (Book 6)

THE OTHER BENNETTS

Controlled Chaos (Book 1)

Finding Chaos (Book 2)

Killing Chaos (Book 3)

Reclaiming Chaos (Book 4)

THE PHANTOM PROTECTORS

Reckless Abandon (Book 1)

Betrayal (Book 2)

Untamed (Book 3)

Guided Loyalty (Book 4)

CARRINGTON-HILL INVESTIGATIONS

Deception (Book 1)

Deadly Desire (Book 2)

SOPHIE MASTERSON SERIES/ DIXON SECURITY

Lifting the Veil (Book 1)

Beyond the Veil (Book 2)

Veiled Intentions (Book 3)

Veiled Threats (Book 4)

THE LOVE FAMILY SERIES

Skylar (Book 1)

Declan (Book 2)

Flynn (Book 3)

Reed (Book 4)

Landon (Book 5)

Alexis (Book 6)

Gabe (Book 7)

Jackson (Book 8)

LINKED INC.

Deadly Intent (Book 1)

Psychic Link (Book 2)

Psychic Charm (Book 3)

Psychic Games (Book 4)

Deadly Dreams (Book 5)

TIME SWEEPERS

Time Watch (Book 1)

Time Keepers (Book 2)

Time Rogue (Book 3)

STAND ALONE READS

Maid of Honor

New Year's Negotiation

Hell Bound

Mystic Tides Box Set

Mystic Luck Box Set

Mystic Kiss Box Set

Karma

Hard Shift

Not My Shifter/ Sinfully Cursed

Made in the USA
Middletown, DE
25 August 2024